WHEN THEY C
An Anthology of

WHEN THEY CAME FOR YOU
An Anthology of Horror Stories

Edited by Dorothy Davies

WHEN THEY CAME FOR YOU
An Anthology of Horror Stories

GRAVESTONE PRESS

A GRAVESTONE PRESS PAPERBACK

© Copyright 2021
Edited by Dorothy Davies

The right of Dorothy Davies to be identified as compiler and editor of this work has been asserted in accordance with the Copyright, Designs and Patents Act 1988.

All Rights Reserved

No reproduction, copy or transmission of the publication may be made without written permission.

No paragraph of this publication may be reproduced, copied or transmitted save with the written permission of the publisher, or in accordance with the provisions of the Copyright Act 1956 (as amended).

Any person who does any unauthorised act in relation to this publication may be liable to criminal prosecution and civil claims for damages.

ISBN: 978 1 78695 641 5

Gravestone Press
is an imprint of
Fiction4All
www.fiction4all.com

This Edition
Published 2021

Even when you're dead you shouldn't lie down and let yourself be buried.
Gordon Lee

Learn when you're dead something like the dawn until let yourself be buried.

Gordon Lee

CONTENTS

Abduction -Dan Allen
Susurrus – Jim Dyar
Death Dealers – Nicole Givens Kurtz
Earth And Smoke And Iron - Sandra Davies
Bitten - Olivia Arieti
Last Stop - Justin Boote
The Song of the Sea - Rie Sheridan Rose
Night Vision – Wendy Lynn Newton
When the Night Bus Comes – David Turnbull
The Price of Ignorance - Wondra Vanian
Maggoty Jo – Diane Arrelle
When The Devil Knocks - Olivia Arieti
Journey Into Darkness – Stuart Holland
To Die For – Chris Rodriguez
Gilded Demons – Terrie Avery
The Gypsy's Curse – Mark Towse
Telling the Bees – Dona Fox
Stealing Souls – Justin Boote
Canvassing - Michael B. Fletcher
Payback – Michael H. Hanson
When They Come For You – Rie Sheridan Rose
Tragic Lullaby – Jim Dyar
Can You Not Smell Them – Dona Fox
Just a Woman - Frances Gow
Devil's Spawn – Diane Arrelle
Sometime in the Small Hours – Gary Budgen

8

Abduction
Dan Allen

Ruth stares at a blank television screen. Yesterday she watched the entirety of *The Sound of Music* this way, even tapping along to the songs and singing when she remembered the words. Today her mind is blank. A slice of soft bread sits in an unplugged toaster. A tea bag rests at the bottom of a cup of cold water. If this is breakfast, the old woman has lost interest.

The phone rings and Ruth doesn't flinch. The noise is far away and its purpose is not clear. It rings until replaced with a monotone request to leave a message.

"Hello, Mom? You need to pick up the phone. It's me, Joan."

A garbage truck stops in front of Ruth's bungalow. There are banging noises and men arguing. Something crashes on the sidewalk and Ruth grabs the armrest of her rocker. Her fingernails penetrate the wood.

"Please, Mom. Answer the phone."

Ruth doesn't recognize the voice; she believes the words have come from the television.

***

Gunshots, breaking glass and men shouting wake the girl. She looks out the second-floor window and watches a uniformed man throw a torch through a broken window. *Yesterday it was the bookstore,* she says to herself. *Today it's the bakery.* She slides to the floor and hugs her knees. A truck rumbles down the street and screeches to a stop. Hard leather boots stomp over cobblestones, each step sounding synchronized as if choreographed.

The girl dares take another look. Soldiers drag a woman and her child, forcing them into the back of the truck. *Just like the other families,* she thinks. They pull a man from the building and beat him to his knees. *Jacob, the baker.* The girl presses a hand against her heart as if to stop it from breaking. Another soldier in a perfectly fitted black uniform points a pistol at the baker's head. The girl has never seen an officer before, at least not this close, and is mesmerized by the contrast of the bright red armband against the black uniform. She watches his grip tighten on the luger. The baker topples a second before the blast echoes down the street.

The girl covers her ears and screams. She shrieks until her face goes red and tears blur her vision. She takes a breath and covers her mouth. *Did they hear me?* she wonders. *Did I give myself away?*

***

Ruth's skin is paper-thin, her once beautiful legs now fragile sticks, and her teeth abandon her nearly as fast as her memories. She has no idea how old she is but curiously remembers her birth date being in August 1925. What that has to do with her age, she has no clue.

The phone rings again.

"Mom, I'm just calling to remind you that we are picking you up tonight. You'll only need to pack for a couple of days. I'll send the rest of your things over later."

Still dressed in her housecoat and slippers, Ruth watches out the window and stares at a fire hydrant. She slowly shakes her head. *That little girl has been waiting there all day. Parents these days don't deserve children.*

"Mom, pick up. I know you can hear me. We've been over this a hundred times. You're going to like Rosewood Manor. You'll meet lots of new friends, eat great food and wait till you see the games room!"

***

Harshly spoken commands direct the familiar sound of boots running. They come closer and closer. Now at the entrance to her building. *They heard me* she thinks and she stops breathing. Fists pound on the door, someone barks orders and the soldiers demand entry. Her flesh freezes as if covered in ice. She knew this day would come but still isn't prepared. *Hide. Now!* The girl squeezes behind a massive armoire; her petit body starved thin enough to make it possible.

Wood splinters and breaks. She flinches at the sound of the front door crashing against the wall. Footsteps thunder up the stairs. The girl tries to count how many. *Two? Six? No, at least ten soldiers. More than enough to find me.* She misses her mother and recites a prayer.

The soldiers make a lot of noise, running from room to room. They yell at each other, not in her language, but she knows it well enough to understand. There's another noise, like a hush. Seconds later, the soldiers retreat. Everything is quiet, but the girl doesn't relax. *It's a trick,* she tells herself. *There wasn't as much thumping on the stairs. They haven't all left.* She holds her breath, afraid to make a sound. Something tickles her foot and she watches a spider crawl over her toes. She sucks in more air, good on top of bad and her chest cavity expands. A button from her sweater snags and pops off. The glass disc *plinks* on the first bounce then rolls out from under the armoire, sounding louder than a handful of marbles on a hardwood floor.

"What do we have here?" The man speaks with a thick accent. An accent that causes her skin to crawl every time she hears it. "Come out from behind there, little gutter rat."

***

A banging sound wakes Ruth and she gasps. An old fear rushes through her veins like a shot of adrenalin. She hears her front door open and her hands tremble. A single thought flashes in her mind. *Hide.* She slides into the broom closet, not quite fitting and leaves the door ajar.

"I got the bedroom. Check the kitchen."

"Got it."

"Here she is, Joan."

Light floods the closet and a hand grabs her wrist.

"Come, Mother. It's time to go. Rosewood is a beautiful place."

Ruth looks into the eyes of her captor and doesn't know the woman. She braces her knee against the doorframe. The stranger tugs her arm and it twists. Ruth's old wrinkled skin stretches and sees the tattoo. The blue numbers are faded but still readable. Ruth screams.

Susurrus
Jim Dyar

It was one freaking God damn fantastic deal and for Bartholomew "Bear" Kowalski, it was going to make him freaking rich.

The tires on the sports utility vehicle squealed as if for joy as Bear hit the on-ramp north with six Grande cups of high-priced iced coffee and the dedication needed to chase the title of prime developer in a state like Maine, full of little people.

"No Jerry, it's the God damn truth," Bear exclaimed drenching his Bluetooth mike with coffee and spit. "Thanks to Covid, these hicks don't know what the hell they're sitting on!"

Jerry's eye roll could be detected in the tone of his voice.

"So, you need a loan."

"Hell, no," Bear snapped. "I need a partner to go in on this. Look, Jerry, everyone's buying up parts of this state and making a serious killing! These are dangerous times and people want to be safe. They deserve to be safe! And the greatest thing is, their money goes a lot further on land up here. We get sixty acres, slap on some condos, people will be screaming for it."

"Just like in Jersey," Jerry sighed. "Massachusetts and what was that place with the two sell-out Marxists? The one that thinks ice cream should come with a java bean enema?"

"Hey, Vermont has more than ice cream," Bear enthused.

"You're right, it has a quick escape to Canada," Jerry responded. Ice clinked on the other line.

"Hey, you drinking again?"

"That implied I stopped the first time," Jerry responded sourly.

"Hah! You got that right! So, we good?"

Jerry was quiet for a minute. The drink was warming his cold personality. Cracking the ice a little bit.

"What's the spread?"

"If we play our cards right, we can get eighty to a hundred times our initial investment. This whole state is like farming money."

Despite some good drinks and a great deal of skepticism, Jerry was intrigued. After listening to a few more minutes of land buyer pitch, Jerry set the glass down on his end table with a solid thud.

"Fine. Fine. Fine. Go do your land grab. The money will be in your bank in an hour."

"Thanks man, you won't regret this."

"And Bear?"

"Yes, mi amigo?"

"Don't let this go all South Philly on me. That put a serious strain on our friendship."

"I won't, Jerry. Sit tight. I got this. Heading there now."

Bear hung up the phone and shifted the vehicle into high gear, just as the first flakes of snow began to hit his windshield and die.

***

Two hours of solid driving, one bathroom pit-stop and four more iced coffees found Bear traveling into the heart of a snowstorm. Light fluffy flakes obscured the forlorn lights of whatever small collection of humanity called this a city. It was mostly a 'blink and you miss it sort of place', even for a state capital. Bear finished tanking up and took off north.

The coffee helped but the going was dark. The entire state of Maine seemed to hold a moratorium on street signs, billboards and other methods for finding out where the hell he was. The only thing he could see for guidance was the occasional sign for i-95 and every once in a while the road was interrupted by another vehicle.

Out of desperation, he flipped on the radio. Some stations were lost in the static of the snowstorm, fading out like galaxies receding. They gave stray hints of speech amongst the crunching of static. When he crossed the fifth full hour of driving, he was down to one lone country and western station, cheerfully twanging out music from long-dead performers and pretending Merle Haggard and Chris Ledux could be called back to perform on a whim.

Even though the snow wasn't accumulating much, it was still difficult to make out the road with the lack of streetlights, city lights, or any lights at all.

Bear was saddle sore from a bucket seat and all the coffee his cup holders could stand. He pulled off to the side of the road to take a much-needed leak.

He whizzed down the embankment behind the SUV with a sigh of relief. It was as he zipped up he heard it.

At first he thought he was still going to the bathroom, but a check later said his hands were still cold. He walked around the vehicle, thinking he could have sworn there were whispers from deep below the range of hearing.

For the first time in his life, Bear regretted those vocabulary lessons he'd taken so he could sound more professional when pressing the flesh.

Susurrus. A gentle whispering wind. Only out here in this night it didn't sound so gentle. It never sounded so sinister when he'd first rolled the word off his tongue, but that was mid-summer, in a safe warm room, deep behind technology's wards.

Carefully he reached in and turned the engine off to listen.

The night was quiet. Amazingly so. In that deep quiet space beyond the wind, Bear could almost hear the sounds of snowflakes sliding over branches, leaves and pine needles, ending the near-perfect silence with a hint of stray movement. He stood listening for several impossibly long minutes.

To a man who'd grown up in a city and lived in cities his whole life, he found it more than disquieting. It was a strange, maddening feeling like the world was waiting for him to make a move and break the silence keeping the darkness in check.

"Damn," Bear muttered under his breath. Even that was loud and shocking, like a gun going off. Unable to shake the melancholy, he climbed into his vehicle and turned the key.

***

The snow had become a clear and present danger not more than an hour or so later. He'd had to slow down to find the road and whatever signs were visible were just ghostly placards with any symbol you wanted to imagine plastered to it. Whatever directions they would have given was reduced to colorless indifference.

More radio stations had come in whilst he was driving, more lonesome cowboy blues, but the disturbing feeling hadn't left him. It had settled in his bones and not even the persistent sounds of ice pellets rattling on the windshield like skeletal teeth, or the persistent rumble of the engine, would dislodge it.

Bear had almost reached the point of slapping his face when a plow truck pulled onto the interstate just ahead of him. It wound slowly around the roads with a soothing rumble and the scrape of metal against asphalt.

He followed it for many miles, comforted by the fact that someone else was alive in the world. Bear was lulled so deep that he lost track of time, even reaching out to turn off the radio absentmindedly when the last station faded beyond the reach of mortal ears.

Then stupor ended abruptly as the mighty plow truck shifted to the left lane and took a sharp turn, leaving Bear to fend for himself. It stung like a betrayal as he lost what he'd considered his angel. The only proof that he wasn't alone in a world of whispering creatures perched and watching among the trees that were pretending to be dead.

`Bear slapped himself in the face.

`"Enough of that shit," he snapped, angry at himself. A cold Maine night was no place to go existential.

But even this bravado faded as he glanced in his rear-view mirror and watched the lights of the plow truck fade behind him.

Light was not merely the absence of dark, but with it gone the emptiness rushed back to overwhelm him.

Bear was starting to think about turning back, but Bangor could not be that far ahead. It wasn't that far north. Even slowed to a crawl he should have found it by now.

He sneaked a peek at his phone but there was no signal. Even his map app couldn't find his location.

Fear stabbed at him as he watched the side of the road for mile markers. As much as he dreaded it, he was going to have to step out of the SUV and find out what mile he was at.

He got out trembling, made his way to the metal post and cleaned the snow from it.

Carefully he did the math, then began whimpering.

Bear was at mile marker 287. He'd missed Bangor hours ago.

The whispering grew louder.

It was different now. He could feel it.

It... They knew where he was and he didn't. He was at their mercy.

He slipped twice on his way back to the van. He had to get turned around and drive back.

He had to make it back to Bangor or this would have been for nothing.

He tried to coax a bit more speed, whilst staring at the unbroken tree line keeping him trapped in the northbound lane.

Trees. Too many trees.

He was unable to see an access road so he spun his vehicle into the tree line where he thought he saw a break between the white bony fingers stabbing at the lightless sky.

The SUV groaned and moaned as it plowed through brush and branches. A metallic crunch signaled he'd hit a rock, but he no longer cared. He had to get away from that awful noise.

More scrapes later he was in the southbound lane and heading back to the last town he remembered being on the map. The vehicle was much louder now and he briefly wondered if he'd lost his muffler, but he was grateful for the extra noise,

He stared out into the frosty night, numbed by the silence. He was trying to get speed back but knew he was pushing it. All he could do was drive. All he needed to do was drive. His vision started to blur.

"You aren't going to get me," he whispered to the noise outside the vehicle.

It was getting harder to breathe, Bear screamed his defiance anyway.

"I SAID YOU ARE NOT GOING TO GET ME!!"

He gasped for air as his vehicle slowed to a stop. He tried to push his foot on the pedal but in response, it sputtered and died.

"I said…" Bear managed again as he stared out the windshield.

The sky seemed to light up, revealing a snowy landscape in which every tree glowed like giant Fey creatures wearing mantles of frosty diamonds. All standing. All staring.

All judging.

Sweat poured from Bear's face in the cooling air. He stared, unable to move.

The susurrus stopped.

Now there were no barriers keeping him from hearing the trees.

***

A long-haul truck driver from Fredericton found the SUV the next morning, deeply frosted with ice, parked on a raised ridge of I-95. State troopers were dispatched but had to wait for the driver's hands to thaw enough to remove them from the wheel. Several false starts later they had the frozen corpse of Bartholomew Kowalski in the body bag and started to zip it shut. They pulled the zipper towards the horrible rictus which his face revealed; it cut off the smell of expensive coffee, the stench of excrement…

And the scent of pine.

Death Dealers
Nicole Givens Kurtz

The wind howled as Trixie and Fox yanked their hoods over their heads and stepped onto the gravel road. The truck driver roared past, spraying apathy and debris. Trixie adjusted her braids into a low ponytail beneath her hood, before hugging Fox to her. The mountains reached for the night sky, decked out in diamond-like stars. The velvety evening heaven had been decorated as if in celebration of their arrival.

"Nobody wants us." Fox shrugged out of her embrace. Her younger brother was already taller than her and teetered in the awkward stage between child and man. His words pinched her heart.

She hugged him close. "Then we'll have us. You build a home out of people, not places." Trixie linked her arm through his. Despite the scowl he wore, she saw him grin quickly before allowing it to dissolve again.

"We'll rise from the ashes of our past." Trixie patted him on the back.

"Uh huh. Covered in soot."

A small chapel rose out of the dust. Trixie headed there as the Arizona sky opened up and rain fell hard and fast. They ran to the worn old door and hid there from the raging squall as best they could. The tiny archway provided little cover as the rain pelted them.

"Can't you do somethin'?" Fox shouted above a clap of thunder.

Trixie sighed. "It's just a little water."

"I'm drownin' standin' up!"

Trixie placed her palm against the wood and concentrated. She could feel the molecules accelerate faster. The wood crackled and buckled beneath the fire. She burned a big enough gap in the door so she could stick her hand in and unlock it.

"Come on!" She pulled Fox inside.

Mold, dampness and desert odors collected in the chapel's stuffy air. The pews sat in neat rows. Fox picked up one of the tiny tealight candles and passed it to her. She lit all three rows of candles, including the one in Fox's hand, with a snap of her fingers. Her powers had grown since the Flagstaff forest fires.

"Trix!" he shouted, startled by her actions. He placed it with the others before turning back to her. "You could've burned me."

She looked back over her shoulder. "No. I've got better control now."

Fox inclined his head, but thankfully did not push the matter. Trixie wiped the ash from her hands and looked around. The tiny chapel had been deserted. Dust bunnies and layers of sand covered everything. Not that the conditions meant anything. In the desert, dust and sand covered everything, except in Phoenix.

She would dust off the ashes of her past.

"Doesn't look like anyone's been blessed in this place in a while."

"It's a blessing for us, then isn't it?" Trixie picked up a hymn book. Its jacket had been worn down to the cardboard inside.

Fox quirked an eyebrow at her. "I guess so."

She paused at the hesitation in his voice. Fox's locks, a bright sun-brushed red, provided evidence of their father's Irish lineage. His dark skin spoke to their momma's deep roots in Africa. Like so many in the after-throes of a collapsed country, the genetics didn't matter—only what they could do with their abilities did.

But not in the land of the sun. All were equal there.

"I know it ain't the best of situations but it's the only place for tonight. Tomorrow…"

"…we see the sun." Fox finished.

She put the book back on the pew.

Fox tossed his hood back and his long dreadlocks spilled over his shoulders. His eyes glowed in the evening's gloom. "It ain't gonna be no different there. Nobody wants us. Too dangerous."

Trixie plopped down onto the first pew and conjured fire from her palm. She held it high as she searched around her immediate area. Fatigued, hungry and crashing from the adrenaline waning in her veins, Trixie couldn't quite put her mind on the right words to ease Fox's fear.

"All are welcomed there. You remember those stories of emancipation we read on the Internet? Of the Israelites out of Egypt? Of the Africans who escaped slavery to the North?"

She closed her eyes and forced the flames in her hand to recede. Her palm stung, but she didn't bother to check it, not anymore. Her hands carried the blackened char of ash. The doctors and scientists couldn't stop that. The tests, the surgeries and numerous drugs all failed to eradicate it.

A genetic oddity.

Magician.

Freak.

Nigger.

She rolled over onto her side. None of the labels meant anything in Phoenix. Everyone could take flight.

"I bet that place ain't seen nothin' like us." Fox huffed. He kept trying to find something identifiable, some *adjective* that would make him fit in a world obsessed with identifying everything and shoving it into its proper place.

"We *are* dangerous, Fox. And tired. Well, I am." Trixie stretched out on the pew and folded her hands behind her head. Her thick frame didn't fit entirely on the narrow wood, but she made it work. Her hoodie served as an adequate pillow.

"Maybe we wouldn't be dangerous if they hadn't kept us like animals in that—that place," Fox said.

The pew behind her creaked beneath Fox's weight. Books, no doubt the hymnals, hit the floor with a series of *thuds*.

"Fox…"

"All right. Lettin' go, sis."

She smiled. "Goodnight, Red."

"I'm a man, not a color."

She giggled as sleep approached. His complaints at her teasing meant Fox hadn't lost all of his innocence and youth—yet.

***

The smack of the chair forced Trixie to jump awake with a shriek. She had been startled from her slumber and fell on the floor with a crash. Worn, frayed carpet had muffled some of the sound, but Trixie had been spooked. Her elbow was smarting and she had a full-on grimace as she got to her feet.

What the hell?

They weren't alone. She stood with her hands aflame and her temper even hotter. "Who are you?"

A large man dressed in a black robe stood across from her. White-blonde shoulder-length hair and cold azure eyes loomed beneath the cloak's hood.

"Hello?" Trixie stepped in front of the pew where Fox had just sat up.

"Trix?" Fox yawned from behind her.

"Who are you?" Trixie positioned her hands.

She took in everything in flashes. The brightness of the chapel. The silence of the people. The scent of something *other* in the air. The hush from outside. Last night, the chapel had been abandoned. No signs of life at all, but then—in her exhaustion and in the gathering dark–she could have miscalculated.

"Hey! She's talkin' to you!" Fox pulled himself up to his full height.

The man in the robe faced them. He threw back his hood and nodded in Fox's direction. "You aren't headed for the sun, are you?"

"Who are you again?"

"The sun is a funny thing. It attracts with its beauty and warmth. It also kills with those same qualities."

When he spoke, it thundered, like a powerful waterfall. The hairs on her neck rose at the man's sheer power. Fear gnawed at the edge of Trixie's courage. What was he?

"Oy, we asked ya first." Fox's glowing eyes shifted to her and then back to the man.

Trixie lowered her hands and mentally extinguished their fire. If this escalated, Fox could get hurt.

"I'm sorry. We trespassed on your property." Trixie picked up her pack.

The man nodded again. "Apology accepted."

"We didn't see no sign. Nothin'." Fox added.

The leader in the cloak had taken several small steps toward them but halted at Fox's words.

"So, uh, who are you?" Trixie asked. She adjusted her hoodie as she walked closer to Fox. If they had to make a run for it or fight their way out, she wanted to be within arm's reach of him.

She wouldn't let anything come between her and freedom. To be her true self. She'd rise above.

"My name is of no importance. What I do, now? That, Trixie and Fox, is what matters most."

"How do you know our names?" Trixie took several steps back.

The man flashed strong white teeth. The smile lacked warmth. "One death dealer knows another."

Trixie tightened her hands into fists. *Death dealer*. No one had called her that, not since the lab.

"I don't deal in death." Not anymore.

"No?"

"No."

Bleary-eyed, hungry and threatened, Trixie struggled with indecision. The stranger's intense watching made her want nothing more than to bolt, to run—or burn the entire place down to the ground.

The latter sounded much better. She'd show them death. Inside her, the other voice that wanted to ignite the very tattered fibers of the world and watch it be devoured by her fury and outrage awoke. Her palms itched and she uncurled her hands, raising them.

Yes, she would show them all how to frighten, to harass with power, to be victims, like so many of her people had been victims—of dogs, chains, whips, spitting, beatings, lynchings… and police sanctioned murder.

"Let's push on, Sis." Fox whispered behind her.

Fox.

The fact he remained, standing beside and depending on her, wrenched her back from the edge. He forced her fury to recede.

She thought of rising on new wings. They were above petty revenge. Freedom waited.

Trixie swallowed the acidic taste on her tongue and backed away from the man and his troop. He remained standing, his pink face shining as if he were sweating hard. His bulk. His voice. His unrelenting stare had nothing on the creepiness and the iciness of his smile.

And he kept grinning as she stepped through the chapel door.

Once outside, Fox yanked up his hood. "What the hell?"

"Let's just go." Trixie started toward the mountains again. "We need to find some food."

Death dealer.

She hadn't heard that term in, well, since the first time they'd escaped from the lab. Death trailed them, like a powerful and expensive perfume that lingered in the room once you'd already left. The bodies in their wake hadn't all been their fault. Still, it lingered in her. The redhead nurse who kept screaming as the lab burned around them, her hair aflame, her eyes wide with agony... *death dealer*.

Trixie shuddered.

"You all right, Trix?" Fox came over to her.

"Yeah. Fine." She tried to put the memory away, but the woman's screams echoed deep into her psyche. Phoenix would burn it out. Then she'd stop hearing them. Now, the desert quiet amplified the memories. "We've got to get to the city. Get food. Get water."

In the faraway distance the metallic and mirrored city buildings reflected the sunlight and sparkled. A new day lumbered on. Trixie shook her head as the heat raged around them. They'd never make it by walking, not in this heat. Her legs kept moving forward despite the truth in her logic.

The chapel grew smaller and smaller behind them. No one had come after them. It felt strange.

So many had chased them. Followed them around stores, around neighborhood, and around the lab.

Watching. Just like that man in the robe.

Most of her life Trixie had known only three things: Struggle. Fight. Run.

Despite the danger that wearing hoods invoked, they had yanked them on. It made it hot. Sure, it deflected some of the sun's rays, but the fabric had been crafted for colder climates.

"Who was that guy?" Fox asked, his face partially shielded by his hood.

"Dunno." Trixie kept walking.

"He knew us." Fox shouted.

"He knew our names." Trixie added.

"More than we got on him, huh?" Fox looked at her and with a shrug, turned back to the road.

"We need a ride." Trixie wanted to put as much distance between her and the man as she could. Something about him left her unsettled. She hadn't come all this way to meet her death and neither had Fox.

***

Weeks later

Trixie crossed into Phoenix proper and the man in the cloak didn't follow. She watched through the sliver of window blinds, but nothing seemed amiss in the pristine, perfect days of life in paradise. Manufactured air pumped through the domed in metro area. The bustling city had been contained from urban sprawl. To Trixie's dismay, the rising bird had been caged.

She stepped out of the adobe home they shared. Over the last two weeks, her alarm had lessened. They were settling into an uncomfortable, but not unpleasant, existence. Trixie struggled with the newness of it all. Clean streets. Free food rations. Air conditioning. No poverty. No politics.

"No peace," Fox remarked, spooking her from behind.

She closed the blinds. "What?"

He tapped his temple. "No peace in here."

"This place is perfect." Trixie gestured to the tranquil scene just outside the windows. "No violence. No trash. Quiet. Even the vehicles are hushed."

They'd been accepted into the city as prelims. Their citizenship relied on how they contributed to the overall progress.

Fox shifted. "Yeah. Too quiet. There's no laughter, talkin', or arguin'."

"You miss the noise? The conflict? The fighting?"

"No, but..."

"Then it's perfect."

He frowned. "The air has an aftertaste."

Trixie sighed. It did.

"So, it isn't perfect. What if I go out and yell?" Fox walked to the door. It hushed open.

"Fox. We been through this. Regulations. This is quiet time."

"My point."

With that, he retreated to his room, a tight triangle corner of their adobe. Once they became full citizens, they'd get a bigger space.

Trixie gazed out over the neighborhood from the open door.

"Ah, there you are." The voice slithered around the sidewalk curve.

Two weeks he'd waited.

The Gringo.

She and Fox had discovered others who spoke of the pale cloaked man they'd met at the chapel, the one who had called himself a death dealer. He'd been called The Gringo, yet no one knew his real name—only his lethal punishment for people who dealt in death, an avenging angel of sorts.

"Your handiwork, excuse the pun, is stamped all over this sector, Trixie."

Trixie narrowed her eyes as he faced her. Her palms itched in anticipation. "What the hell do you mean?"

The Gringo laughed. "Don't you smell it? The fear your presence generates?"

"We'll call the police! Get out of here!" Fox took out his phone.

The man tossed a fireball at Fox. Trixie screamed and dove in front of the hurling flames. The heat blew through her, singeing her eyebrows, brushing her face.

She scrambled to her feet and set her own palms on fire. The Gringo had encroached on their yard. *Who is this guy?*

"The Gringo has powers."

"No kidding!" Trixie leapt back into the door. It closed, slicing off the sound fight.

32

Fox panted a few feet away. Already his shape threatened to shift. His eyes glowed scarlet and his knuckles curled into the beginnings of paws.

"No, Fox!" She hurried to calm him. Across from the door, his serum sat on the table, amber liquid in capped syringes. Trixie snatched the cap off of one and slammed it into his buttocks.

He howled in alarm and raced off through the house.

Outside, the Gringo continued his assault. Glass shattered. The scent of burning vegetation wafted inside.

"What do you want?" she shouted through the open door.

Blue and red lights spilled in. The police had arrived.

"Citizens. Desist your use of powers," a disembodied voice commanded. Disrupting the sanctioned quiet time was a serious offense.

Trixie crawled over broken glass and shattered furniture, some still smoking.

She and Fox had been chased across the southwest. Hunted. Then it clicked. Him.

"Fox! We have to get out of here! Find the sanctuary and plead for amnesty."

Fox was pressed against the wall, drenched in sweat. His nose had elongated into a snout. He barked. "What? Now?"

"The Gringo!"

Damn. The serum injection had come too late and he'd already begun to change. Trixie sprinted around the room, snatching up their few possessions and tossing them into her satchel. Her hands shook.

"The Gringo?"

Trixie stopped. "I—I didn't think he really existed. Urban legend. Vapors. Remember Denver?"

Denver had been before Flagstaff.

Clean streets. Hushed quiet during daylight hours. Domed paradise. She'd been a fool. A gullible fool.

Freedom.

Before she could explain, the front door blew off its track. The Gringo came in, grinning.

"Out! Out! Damn black spots!"

"Spots?" Fox barked as he shifted to a sizable red fox, losing all ability to speak.

"Stains on the lovely purity of this city. I will make it clean." The Gringo grinned and rapidly threw fireballs at them.

"Run, Fox!" Trixie deflected the attack with fire of her own.

The Gringo moved fast and, before long, had her by the throat. He threw her outside and she slammed into the manufactured lawn. It flickered as the hologram program crashed, revealing a section of dark gray plasma screen.

"Worthless. Designer scientists' cheap experiments." The Gringo grabbed both her wrists when she tried to defend herself.

"Run, Fox!" she shouted again.

Overhead, a crisp blue sky and lemonade sun rested in the heavens. When she looked closely, she could see small reflections against the clear dome. Picture. Perfect. So quiet. No peace.

"You sought freedom." He laughed.

Trixie screamed as his hands burned the flesh around her wrists. Agony flowed through her. He had set her skin on fire. The burning flames funnelled out of his palms and scurried up her arms.

"Yes! Scream out your pathetic soul. If you bastards have one."

Trixie collapsed as he let go. Had it all come down to this? The fight? The struggle? All in vain.

She pushed back with flames of her own, fire against fire with her body the battlefield. The Gringo's powerful flames roared; his hatred fuelled.

Agony wore through her anger, leaving only emptiness. Her fire quieted as she slumped to the ground.

The Gringo's grin was wide and cold. "Die."

Trixie shivered as her flame retreated, worn down by the Gringo.

Then, ripping through the afternoon's polished peace, a fox howled in the distance.

Now, it was her turn to smile. Warmth came and grew hotter.

She didn't scream as the agony of fire crackled along her flesh, her hair, her sight.

For like a phoenix, Trixie would rise.

Earth And Smoke And Iron
Sandra Davies

It were an odd one and no mistake. *She* were odd. Educated; not from round here. 'Otherworldly' some might say.

She lugged it in, wrapped up in brown paper, tied with string. Knots sealed with blobs of scarlet wax.

'You'll 'after tell me what's in it, lass –'

'A coat. An army one. That's what's the smell –'

I sniffed. And aye, beyond the paper there was earth and smoke and iron. 'Who's is it?'

'It's Paul's – He'll need it when he comes. I've told him I'll leave here, to collect.'

'And when's this Paul coming for it, lass?'

'Soon. He said soon –'

Her face all aglow in an expectation I hoped would not be broke. Seen too many o' them over the last few years. 'I'd best 'ave your name, lass. And an address.'

That fazed her. Didn't want to say but couldn't bring herself to tell a lie.

'It's Leonie,' she whispered.

The address she gave was the pilot's cottages, down at the tip of Spurn Point. Last time I was there they were ugly black-tarred wooden huts. Three or four mebbe, but no place for a lass like this one.

Like a crystal glass in the roughest sailors' dive.

Weeks went past. No-one came. No surprise. Then I met Meg Partridge in the street. She a pilot's wife. Built like a tank, six bairns in five years and stood no nonsense. I asked her, 'D'you know a Leonie? Married to a Paul?'

Her face rolled a somersault from scorn to pity and back again. '"Paul"? Her man's John Cooper –'

'Brother, then?'

'She's no-one else. John rescued her. Vicar's daughter, didn't know owt about anything. When John took her – and he'd put himself to the trouble of wedding her first! – damned near screamed the place down, John said. 'E's besotted. Made a promise to a dying man to look after her. Guess that could be Paul.'

'If no-one comes for it soon I'll 'after let it go. Can you tell him to come and fetch it?'

John Cooper wasn't best pleased.

'There's no such coat, 'cept in her imagination, which has Paul wrapping her in it on the beach every bloody night.'

'Best we open it to make sure –'

But sure enough, all there was was the smell of earth and smoke and iron.

'Iron?' John Cooper said. 'That's the blood he shed before he died.'

Bitten
Olivia Arieti

The angels had trouble preparing the baby for his birth. The fairness of the hair turned dark just like the eyes, the countenance was exceedingly restless and the wings indispensable for the return trip, would stick no way on the back. The event occurred in one of the remotest chambers of Hawkedge Manor, an isolated mansion where the mother, a lovely noble lady, had dwelled since her marriage. A tormented story marked her romance with its owner who had induced her to abandon the paternal house and marry him. The girl never regretted it, but had to adjust to her new life, totally dedicated to satisfy the whims of her arrogant and capricious sire. Yet his love was so complete, his admiration so strong and passion intense that she felt the most exclusive and precious being in the world. After long absences, he would appear in the middle of the night, wake her up and his hands would set her body aglow, while his kisses were ardent enough to make her bleed.

Sadly, her delicate constitution didn't sustain the fatigue and bearing a child was the final blow that subtracted her from the world a few minutes after the baby, Richard, came into it.

A cadaverous nanny took care of him and of his cousin, Beth, who arrived a few months later.

Late one evening, a strange dark being accompanied the child to the door and, after a hasty farewell, he and his carriage vanished into the darkness.

The children grew up wandering in the surrounding woods, swimming in the nearby lake and conjecturing about their mysterious parents that neither could remember. They would often be confined to the library where Sir Blair, a most austere tutor, took care of their education. His lessons also included subjects like black magic, the occult and paranormal science that inevitably kindled the fantasy of his pupils, now and then struck by strange reminiscences or weird feelings without any reasonable explanation.

Sir Blair lodged in the tower where a small chamber had been given over to him. The servants were diffident and used to withdraw when he passed by. The nanny spent some time with him and everyone in the household had the impression they were old friends. More than once they were seen together in the park at night, heading towards the gate before being swallowed by the mist.

Strangely, it was after one of these nights that the news of a sudden illness or an inexplicable death was spread the following day. A maidservant, rosy cheeked Lilian, fell suspiciously ill shortly after her arrival. The housekeeper had replaced the nanny and Sir Blair entered her room at midnight quite often, when moans were heard by the other servants. The lass quickly turned pale and, a few weeks later, died.

Beth and Richard grew up restless and introverted as if an obscure melancholy had darkened their spirits. Less time was spent together as Richard detested his cousin's grim interests; she insisted on being accompanied for long walks that always ended at the village's graveyard as though responding to a macabre attraction she couldn't resist.

The boy had developed an inclination to solitude; apparently, an obsessive malady was pricking his soul. Lugubrious shadows filled his room, making his nights sleepless; or he would suddenly leap up, overwhelmed by an uncontrollable craving for wandering around till the crack of dawn.

New neighbours visited them one late autumn day. Lord William, a widower, had inherited Whiteridge Hall, a nearby property, and moved there with his siblings, George and Maureen. Richard was breathless on seeing the girl, fatally attracted as a rabid bee by the sweetest flower. Since the nobleman was often away on business, the visits were intensified as the youths didn't like remaining alone in a house still so unfamiliar to them.

When a furious storm arrived, brother and sister were forced to stay with their hosts for a few days as trees had been uprooted and the road was interrupted by their trunks.

The rain kept falling heavily and the place looked gloomier than usual.

After dinner they gathered in front of the fireplace, the fire by now dying and unable to dissipate the dampness of the room.

"It's quite creepy in here," said Maureen.

"I don't think I'll like living in this part of the country," added her brother. A sudden flare made everyone cover their eyes.

"Better go to bed," he said. "I heard that spirits love roaming around on nights like this." He quickly bid everyone goodnight.

Beth's glance followed him; her eyes were red and her lips curled in a rapacious grimace.

"Wait, George," she cried, "let me go with you," and ran after him.

A terrified expression showed on her cousin's face, but he did his best to mask it.

"I like you, Richard," said Maureen, softly.

Dismayed by her straightforwardness, he remained silent for a while. Then he took her hands and was about to kiss them when something sharp pierced his tongue. He pulled her towards him, this time willing to kiss the lips but, overwhelmed by his own rapture and by the intensified feeling of the piercing, stepped away.

"I bet you wanted to bite me," she giggled and pulled back her chestnut curls leaving her neck visible.

Richard was speechless. Fright and a sudden thirst seized him. What on earth was happening to him? And why did she tempt him so?

"Not tonight, darling," she muttered alluringly and left the room.

The bitter taste in his mouth induced him to wipe his mouth with his handkerchief; red stains tainted its whiteness. His tongue was bleeding.

Nightmares, hallucinations and thirst did not leave Richard that night. He poured himself a glass of brandy, but it didn't help. Maureen's scent was still with him. He wondered if that was love, but there was a certain wantonness, an insane pleasure that stirred his senses, an unfamiliar yearning to taste her blood… the infamous urge to bite.

Had he become a demon? The idea frightened him to the point that he ran to stand in front of a mirror to see if horns had sprouted from his head, but terrified, he stepped back on not finding any image.

The horrid truth fell upon him like the blow of an axe. He was a vampire, the nefarious uncanny creature that had haunted him since his birth. Immediately he realised that the house was full of bloodsuckers and Beth, Sir Blair and his own nanny ranked among them.

Lilian also flashed before his eyes, her emaciated face the reflection of the continuous draining of her blood till death. Was she, too, still searching for fresh bodies?

He wondered why he had been spared till then… Could it have been his mother interceding? At the end, though, she couldn't do anything to end such a hideous lineage.

Whatever, love had awakened his nature, but also sharpened the instinct to safeguard his dearest.

He was flooded by so many considerations, memories and fears, that he felt his head burst with terror, his heart with despair.

The following day, George was ill and his sister spent most of the time by his bedside.

"Where were you last night?" enquired Richard.

"Fast asleep in my room," she replied with an innocent smile.

"Don't you ever try to get close to Maureen or a stake will run through your heart, my dear cousin."

"No threat can scare me, for my powers equal yours," she replied defiantly.

That evening their guest came down to dinner in an elegant white satin dress, adorned with ruffles on the gown and sleeves. Her appearance and scent mesmerised both cousins. Beth kept staring and Richard sensed the vampire's voracity.

"I am sure you want to check on George, Beth," he said firmly, on leaving the dining room, "In the meantime we will take a stroll in the garden." He took Maureen's arm.

"I warned my brother to watch out," she said when they were under the pergola. "He, too, easily loses his head over pretty young ladies, just like you." She surprised him again. Did she know the truth?

"There is something I must tell you…"

The girl put a finger on his lips, "Hush, Richard, hush," then she smiled, "Yesterday I liked you, tonight I love you to the point of…" she paused and with an imploring glance sidled up to him, her breath on his face…

Once again, his throat was on fire, the yearning for blood driving him out of his senses, but he had to resist. He clenched his teeth, swallowed the flames of hell and pushed her away.

"I want you to leave the manor tonight, and never to come back again."

Like a wild animal he was fighting against his own instinct if ever it might have been possible... He was trembling, aching, yearning to flee before it was too late.

How long would love be able to master temptation?

Maureen took his hand, the touch as soothing as a maternal caress.

"My brother is already part of your family, let me join in too."

"Why, dear, why?"

"I just told you, sweetheart," she said and added, " trust me, I am brave enough to endure whatever will happen as long as you keep me with you."

Richard was devastated. It would have been useless persuading her to leave. He was the one who had to go, but how could he abandon her there with the ravenous Beth and all the others?

"Come, we're off," he said and handed her the cloak.

The carriage dashed wildly across the barren countryside as if transported by demoniac coursers, but Maureen was happy, sure that her dark sire would soon make her his.

The speed was such that the vehicle hit a tree and crashed.

Desperate cries followed; Richard managed to extricate the injured girl and lay her on the damp soil. She was fatally wounded... a few more seconds and she would close her eyes... With her last strength she uttered as if saying an ultimate prayer, "Don't let me leave you, Richard," and her head reclined for the extreme fatigue.

Could love go beyond horror? Nothing mattered any longer. He, too, wanted her by his side, forever, and there was only one way out.

The ability to heal rapidly helped the bloodsuckers to recover fast and return to Hawkedge Manor.

Richard, having gained his dark nature from his father's side only, wasn't as wicked as his similar; besides, his love for Maureen had mitigated his rapacious instinct.

Since blood was essential for survival, however, they had to assure their nourishment.

They picked their prey scrupulously, never separating lovers and always granting them supernatural life together.

Time passed, the mansion decayed and became dreary, but at night it glowed with a ghastly splendour that showed its past dwellers were still there, ready to haunt whoever dared to trespass past the gate.

Last Stop
Justin Boote

"Ah, shit!"

Shaun Thornsley rubbed his eyes and looked around. Confusion was the dominant factor here. Confusion and concern that things might have gone terribly wrong.

His unease turned to dread when he realized he was the only person on the Underground train. This could mean only one thing—he'd fallen asleep and missed his stop. He was tired, hungry and wanted the warmth and comfort that only one's bed could satisfactorily provide, and now that seemed so far away.

He looked down at himself. The contents of a beer can had dispersed all over his lap and there was a suspicion of vomit on his chest as well, plus a small splat by his feet. The taste in his mouth was comparable to rotten vegetables. He threw the empty can on the floor and groaned when his head began throbbing intensely. Another after-work session with the guys gone wrong.

He looked at the time on his phone; three a.m. Yep, this was definitely the last train of the night and he should have gotten off at least twenty minutes ago. He should, in fact, be curled up in bed right now, sandwich and can of beer his faithful companions while watching whatever rubbish was being shown on T.V. until sleep came for him.

"But...?" He stopped midway through the question he was asking himself. If he should have gotten off twenty minutes ago, surely the train would have reached its final destination by now? He looked at the electronic board above the door. His suspicion was confirmed; all the little red lights were flashing, including that of the last station, Belton.

So where the hell was the train going then?

Could it really be that far to wherever trains themselves slept for the night? Or maybe the driver had turned around at the last stop and was going back the way he'd come? That would involve a journey of at least an hour. So why hadn't the driver checked to make sure everyone was off?

He looked along the train. As it headed around corners and sped along, his pounding, dehydrated brain made him think of a giant snake twisting and squirming down some dark and dangerous tunnel, perhaps chasing some unsuspecting prey, or a great, monstrous worm swimming beneath treacherous sands. Not good thoughts to be having when one is stuck on an empty train with a rumbling, equally empty stomach and smelling of vomit and booze.

Another thought crossed his mind and this was also one to add to the list of ominous and disturbing possibilities. They hadn't gone past a single station since he'd awoken. He should have at least seen the lights of the stations as they flashed past, or were they all turned off as well? But didn't the cleaners work the night shift, clearing up all the puke and empty bottles and cans before opening up to the public again? Certainly the train he was on now had its fair share. It was Friday, the bar he worked at had been overflowing with people until closing time and it seemed more than a few had emptied the contents of their stomach and bladder later on the floor. The train stank of piss, alcohol and sweat. And Shaun.

He rose, his legs almost betraying him and staggered against the door. The emergency button was next to it.

"Hey, driver!" he called through the intercom.

No answer came.

"Hey, driver! Can you hear me? Where the hell are we? I want to get off!"

A muffled static was the only response but then, the train began to slow down. Further down the tunnel, finally, he could see a light. A platform!

He gave thanks that he wouldn't be spending the night in this stinking, filthy train and waited for it to enter the station.

The train pulled in. He looked along the platform; it was empty. The only concession that life had ever been here were the empty beer cans scattered irrelevantly despite the garbage bins, and the multiple splats of vomit in varying colours, quantity and composition. Shaun grimaced, thought about how disgusting some people could be, then remembered his own current state and the beer can he had left on the floor as company to the others.

"Fuck it," he mumbled. "That's what the cleaners are for. If it wasn't for people throwing their crap on the floor, they wouldn't have a job. Should be grateful."

The train stopped. He looked at the sign on the platform; Bradwell. Too far for him to walk, but a taxi wouldn't deplete his already severely dented budget. Ten minutes and he'd be home. He waited for the doors to open, but then, movement to his left startled him. A shadow, long and huge and round slowly came into view from the stairs that led onto the platform.

It must be the cleaners after all, he thought, but there was something... unnatural about the shadow. It didn't look like the elongated form of a person; it was too wide and several appendages seemed to be attached to it. Or could it be the mop and broom poles of the cleaner as she came down the stairs?

He looked to his right. Other shadows appeared, some small, others larger yet all bearing a form completely distinct to one another. Then, he took a step back and gasped in disbelief and horror.

The thing had appeared on the platform. The doors to the train were still shut and in his momentary shock he hadn't thought about why, but through the dirty, graffiti-incrusted window the thing looked like some giant cockroach ambling along. It was approximately the size of a large dog—a Rottweiler perhaps—covered in scales and moved on six legs; its bloated body rubbing along the ground, antennae waving in the air above its head.

"What the fuck...?" blurted Shaun. He watched, frozen, as the thing moved from one spot to another apparently eating the beer cans and lapping up the vomit piles.

Another stepped into the light, followed by more strange creatures. All the same size apart from two that were slightly bigger with a red band running down their back, their rounded heads coming to a sharp point at what might have been a chin. These sat and watched the other creatures cleaning up the mess as though dictating orders.

Then the doors opened. The suddenness of it sent Shaun staggering back again, shock sending him reeling to the floor. Footsteps echoed along the platform, accompanied by whistling. He could hear a clicking noise that seemed to follow a pattern, like Morse code; clicks of three followed by a pause then rapid ones of four or five and knew this, with total and horrific certainty, to be the sound of the creatures communicating with each other.

A shadow loomed.

He looked up to see a person standing over him, hands on hips, smiling. He was wearing a blue uniform with the transport company logo on it.

"Well, well. What have we got here, then?"

Shaun looked up, lower jaw resting on his chin, drool dripping onto his chest.

"Cat got your tongue, has it? Better that than the cleaners, eh?"

Shaun could only mouth empty words.

"You messed up big time, son. In more ways than one, actually, judging by the state of you," said the driver, grimacing at the stains on Shaun's shirt.

"You know, I was sure I checked all the wagons thoroughly before turning around. Doesn't do to have people see what really goes on down here at night. Who really has to clean up the mess you dirty little shits leave behind."

The driver tutted and shook his head.

"What are they?" Shaun finally managed.

"Them?" he replied, pointing at the creatures still waddling along the platform.

Shaun nodded.

"They're the cleaners. I told you." He paused. "Ah, I get it. You thought actual people cleaned up all your waste and crap! Well, you're wrong, son. How could you possibly expect another human being to clean up all your puke and piss and God knows what else? So, we… umm… trained a few. A few like you, actually."

The words entered into Shaun's brain but there was very little cohesion or recognition. And what did he mean '*like you*'?

Another shadow slowly came into view accompanied by that clicking sound.

"Ah. Hi there, Phil. Busy night again?"

Shaun let out a squeak of fright and pushed himself away from the open door. The shadow belonged to one of the great insect-things. It crept slowly into the wagon, clawed feet clicking on the wagon's floor, its bloated body squelching as it dragged itself in. It was one of the ones with the red stripe along its back, but this was the least significant thing about it.

Its face was human.

Its features were distorted, but there could be no denying in its eyes that this thing had at one stage, somehow, been a human being. Bloodshot, darting from left to right with no synchronization to them, the irises a dark blue colour. The nose had withered away to a small snub but two nostrils were still present. The mouth was an impossibly wide contraption, full lips—human lips—at breaking point, cracking under the weight of its grin, showing the teeth that were small and plenty and yellowed and terribly sharp. Something slimy and grotesque darted in and out of its mouth that Shaun feared might be a tongue.

"Meet Phil, the foreman," said the driver. "As you can see, he's dedicated to his job. Doesn't mean he likes it, though. Can't blame him I suppose. But then, he brought it on himself. As you did."

This was some stupid, terrible nightmare. Someone had put an acid tab in his drink or something because obviously this wasn't—couldn't—be happening. Or maybe he was still asleep on the train and soon someone would wake him and tell him to get the hell off.

But then, he didn't ever recall being able to smell anything so foul before in one of his habitual dreams. Or feel the way the thing was touching him with its antennae, its tongue darting out to poke at his chest.

Another insect-thing entered the train and began gobbling up the waste on the floor. It came to Shaun and opened its enormous mouth.

"Stop, Mike! That's no way to treat a new workmate. Be a little compassionate."

The thing made a clicking sound with its tongue, backed off and continued down the wagon.

"Well, we better get going. You'll have an interview once we get back to the headquarters, but

I think you'll make a fine employee. You have the right… aptitude, I think. We could do with a few more extras anyway. Just never enough workers to cope with the demand.

"Phil, Mike! Time to go. I'll come and pick you up later."

The two creatures obediently left the train and resumed cleaning the platform while the driver pressed a button by the door closing it instantly.

Shaun sat, huddled against the opposite door, mumbling incoherencies to himself. Nothing made sense, yet at the same time was totally feasible and logical. A paradox of sensibilities. The train began moving along again, occasionally tooting its horn as they passed another station; Shaun not daring—and incapable anyway—of looking onto the platform. He'd seen enough already tonight and feared the worst was yet to come.

He didn't know how it was going to happen, but he had a feeling he'd puked himself into a situation without remedy. By joining the late-night slob brigade, having not a single compassionate thought for those who would have to come behind him and others to clean up the human waste, he had inadvertently created a new career for himself. One that would see him not serving the drinks to fellow slobs but helping to clean up the aftermath. He'd come full circle in providing a service to those that saw the graveyard shift as an excuse to imitate the vermin that lived underground. And now, they had seen him and come for him as one of their own.

The train finally pulled into the last stop and opened its doors. Shaun rose and stepped onto the platform. Giant bugs and scaly things dashed around lapping up waste, chewing on metal cans and glass bottles. Some meandered over to him, their antennae snaking over his legs, opening vast mouths before closing them again and heading off to find other pastures in which to graze.

A moment of clarity sparked a reaction from Shaun. He didn't know what the hell was going on here, but he sure didn't want to be part of it. Some experiment surely—he'd read about such things on the Internet. He looked around until he saw the stairs that led out of the platform and to safety above ground.

He bolted.

He'd almost made it up the first set of stairs when something came around the corner. Such was his momentum that he had no time to react, tripped over the insect-thing and was sent sprawling. The insect hovered over him, a rapid clicking noise coming presumably from its mouth or throat, its tongue feeling its way over his chest and face until the train driver appeared.

"Come on, son. The doors are locked anyway."

The driver picked him up and led him back down again until they came to a door. Above it was a sign; 'Danger! Interview and Processing Room!' He knocked on the door, opened it and peered in.

"Got another one for you, sir."

"Okay, send him in."

The driver looked at Shaun and smiled. "Don't worry, son. Soon, you'll see things from a whole new perspective. Call it a 'cleansing experience'. Put some real effort and dedication into your new job, promotion is always a possibility. Underground stations are not the only places we're contracted by."

With that, he pushed Shaun into the room and slammed the door firmly shut behind him.

***

The After Midnight nightclub closed its doors. Bouncer Steve Watton was relieved. Another night of sweaty, drug-induced, drunken assholes finally gotten rid of. They disgusted him. Puking, pissing on the toilet floor. If they were lucky. Many didn't make it that far. But that was for the cleaners.

He needed a piss himself. He took a deep breath, then barged into the men's room. No point stepping over puke and piss stains to get to the urinal. Might as well piss on the floor. A little more won't bother the cleaners.

As he stood relieving himself, he heard a noise behind him. The door opened and a clicking sound accompanied it. He tensed, some asshole who'd fallen asleep under the stairs, no doubt. But then, a slurping, sucking sound caused his muscles to tighten and his heart to throb madly in his chest. Followed by a voice.

"Well, Shaun. Looks like you might have yourself an apprentice."

The Song of the Sea
Rie Sheridan Rose

The becalmed ship hung suspended in an obsidian glass ocean reflecting a moonless sea of stars. We'd remained adrift near a week now and the captain was on a right old tear, so I made myself scarce up in the crow's nest, figuring it the safest place to be when Black Jack O' Reilly had sought solace in the rum. So, I saw it all—and I will never forget a single moment of that damnable night.

You might well ask how a bilge-water cabin boy got to know words like "obsidian," but this is the story of my last days at sea and why I went back to school and made something of myself as soon as I touched dry land again. I ventured as far inland as I could go and I won't ever go near the water again, I take my oath.

My name is David Phelps, though it was just Davy in those days. A homeless waif who took Black Jack's shilling because it was that or starve. He seemed kind enough—didn't cuff me more than once or twice a day and I was quick to learn what set him off. The rest of the crew were decent sorts, though I soon found out the way of things when we set upon a merchantman my first week at sea.

I hadn't intended to pledge myself to a pirate, but I had, so I accepted my fate, picked up my cudgel and laid about me with the rest.

It was chaos.

I had never been a part of such madness. Pirate and merchant alike, they fought like fiends. The air was rank with the hot smell of gunpowder and the metallic taint of blood. It was soon hard to keep one's feet as the deck grew slimy with gore. The shouts and reports of pistol and rifle were deafening. I wanted to crawl in the hold and hide, but knew that would be worse than standing my ground if Black Jack found me cowering. I'd be off the ship in a heartbeat—and without the benefit of a dory.

So, I fought on. The quarry's crew had not been expecting pirates this close to home and they were dispatched with relatively little effort, despite what it seemed to a boy who'd known nothing of fighting till this very day. The merchant captain—he was another story.

From what I could ferret out much later, he was newly wed and returning home from his marriage trip with his bride before setting her up in a nice, safe establishment with a widow's walk to seek him by. It was the very devil's luck that our ship met his that day. He fought like Ol' Scratch himself, protecting the cabin she hid within.

It only made Jack more determined to have whatever prize he held so dear. I suspect he thought it gold or jewels...but it was instead a ravishing beauty with hair like black silk and skin with a hint of coffee. One look and Jack must have her—no care for the blonde beauty who waited at his own homestead. He ran the captain through and hauled her out of the cabin with hands slick with blood.

Her dark eyes swam with tears as she gazed upon her dead husband, but she never spoke a word. She allowed Jack to drag her back to his own ship, but I knew even then there would be hell to pay for this day's work.

There was a stillness to the ship the next day. The quartermaster split the take and all got a decent share, but it didn't make up for the unease in the air. The shanties that usually filled the workday were silent. The quartermaster as much as whispered his orders.

The wind whispered as well. The ship barely moved—we could see the death ship on the horizon for three days and I just knew we'd be taken for gutting her. Finally, Jack ordered the longboat down and sent men to scuttle her. At least it got her off our bow.

The wind condescended to blow us further from the shipping lanes, but then it died again. It continued that way for weeks—a fitful breeze for a few hours, then dead calm once more—and the woman never said a word to anyone. I would hear Jack railing at her and the sound of blows, punctuated with less savory grunts and groans, but never a word from her lips to a soul. At night, however, when I was sleeping on the deck outside Jack's cabin lest he call me and he dead-to-the-world from rum, I could hear her singing softly, words in a tongue I did not know. The sound was haunting. It would follow me down into my dreams and they became nightmares.

This was the way of things for several weeks, as I said. The woman silent except for her cries of pain and that eerie singing...wasting away before my eyes when I tried to get her to eat something...anything. One night, just before dawn, she looked into my eyes and smiled—a wan, but incandescent smile—and whispered one word. "Leave."

I held her in my arms as she died.

I was ten. I didn't know what to do. There was no way for me to leave—the ship was far from shore. I told the doctor and he threw a bucket of water on Jack to rouse him.

"Your fancy woman is dead, Jack. 'Tis what comes of such things," the doctor told him, his voice cold as the snow.

Jack growled, "Throw the bitch over the side and have done with her."

A nod and she was hauled over wrapped in a stained sheet with a cannonball at her feet.

Sound returned to the ship that day—the bark of orders, the shantyman's squeezebox, the ribald comments among the crew...

It was as if the silence had never descended. No one seemed to find it strange that her passing had brought back the sounds of everyday life... and perhaps I was mad to think it so, but I still cried my eyes red for her poor unshriven soul. Even if no one else seemed to care.

And now, we have returned to where I began...the obsidian sea and the cloudless sky—becalmed far from any shred of land. We hadn't made port in near three months and supplies were beginning to run low... oranges, salted beef and, most dangerously for the crew... the rum. Most could live on watered ale and hardtack, but Jack was fierce when he had no rum. My back wears many a stripe it would not if there had been more rum.

So, as I said, after mess, when my chores were done, I retreated to the crow's nest where I might be safe unless he noticed and then I would be for it no matter what, so it was worth the chance.

I gnawed upon a biscuit, staring out into that starlit night and coming to the realization that the sea might not be the place for me. I was weighing what options I might consider when next we docked when I heard it...

Drifting over the sea like an unseen mist was a sweet, heart-wrenching song that sent a spike of ice right through me. I recognized that voice and the soft cadence of the language I still can't decipher all these years later. It was *her* voice, *her* song...but she was dead. I had been there when the doctor and the quartermaster dropped her over the side of the ship.

I rose to my knees, peeking over the side of the nest and scanning the sea around us. All was as black and featureless as it had been since sunset—but wait! In the distance, a pool of light reflected from the mirrored sea.

As I watched, eyes like to pop from my head, the light came closer and the song grew louder.

I clapped my hands over my mouth to stifle a scream. I could see a figure in that light, walking across the surface of the water like Jesus in the Good Book is said to do.

This was no Savior, however. Instinctively I knew as much. Black hair flowed in an unfelt wind and her bare feet skimmed the water like birds. The winding sheet was gone and the tattered gown mere rags—but it was the merchant's bride. I would swear all I possess on it. She glowed with an inner light and I had never—before or since—seen anything so ethereally beautiful.

But the closer she came to the ship, the greater the unease I felt. Where was the watch? Did no one else see this? Why was there no outcry? I would expect the entire crew to be gawping over the rail at such a sight, and yet, there was nothing.

I rose to my feet, prepared to go down and raise the cry myself, but then she looked up to where I stood and I heard a voice in my head.

"Stay where you stand, or die."

I was not that attached to the crew.

I did as I was told, cowering against the side of the crow's nest like the frightened child I was. But I could not turn my eyes away. She meant me to bear witness.

The singing grew louder, deeper, stronger... as if the sea itself was adding its voice to hers. Other shapes began to form, rising in a mist about the ship. Where the night had been cloudless, without a breath of wind, a heavy fog composed of writhing figures surrounded us now. Summer lightning began to play in the sky.

And now the crew poured onto the deck.

"Davy!" roared Black Jack, "where are you? Devil take you! Bring me my cutlass!"

I decided he could have fetched it up himself if he wanted it and held my peace.

"Light the lanterns!" ordered the quartermaster. "Let's see what we're facing."

Crewmen rushed to obey and the eerie eldritch light coming off the fog was augmented by the warm, familiar light of the bull's-eye lanterns. It didn't change much. There was still nothing tangible to see, just those writhing shapes in the mist... and then she stepped over the rail, as casually as if it were a stick upon the road and not a dozen feet above the water.

Jack frowned. I could see him recognize her in the start back and the pallor that bloomed across his face. "You can't be here," he barked—as if he could order her away. "You're dead and rotting on the bottom of the sea."

She tilted her head, that incandescent smile upon her face and then she began to dance around him, faster and faster, her singing providing the music for her steps.

Jack spun, trying to keep her in sight.

It was almost comical. But as she danced... she began to change. The beauty fell away and her form and features reflected the truth he had given voice to. Her skin sloughed off, revealing ivory bone and leathery sinews and still she danced. Skeletal fingers beckoned and the other shapes in the mist began to take on concrete form. Sailors and soldiers swarmed over the rail. Merchant seaman and navy alike. I saw the merchant captain step to her side and twirl her through a measure of waltz before focusing his attention on Jack.

Every man the pirates had sent to the bottom of the sea in their long and storied career now howled for revenge. They fell upon the crew and began to tear them limb from limb. The merchant captain still clutched a rusty sword in one hand and he split Jack from head to crotch in one fell blow.

And all the while, she kept singing. The haunting lilt of that song now became a screech of triumph as the pirates fell about their victims. Blood ran like water across the deck and into the thirsty sea.

When every living soul upon that ship save one was dead—else how could I sit here and tell you my tale?—she finally fell silent.

She grasped her husband's hand in hers, turned and looked up to where I crouched. "Get you far from the sea," she murmured, in a voice like the call of a dove. "'Tis no place for one such as you. Take what you can carry and lower the dory. You will reach safe landing—but never again will the sea be a haven for you."

I nodded, wide-eyed.

And then, as quickly as they had come, the ghostly shapes faded. The merchant and his lady were last to depart, dancing one final waltz on the bloody deck to her beautiful singing.

Only when they too were gone did I dare descend. Though it was still the dead of night, I did as she had ordered and filled the dory with food, water and enough gold to make my way and lowered the boat.

I rowed away from the ship as quickly as I was able and before I had gotten more than a few dozen yards from her, she went under with a groan of shifting timbers and dead souls. I feared the suction would take me under with her, but I clung to the dory and somehow made it through.

Four days later, with bloody hands and cracked lips, I was picked up by a merchant ship and I made my way eventually to land, vowing never again to set eyes upon the ocean. For fifty years, I've held true to that vow... but some silent nights, I still hear the song of the sea in my dreams.

Night Vision
Wendy Lynn Newton

When you're a shadow hunter, the last place you want to be stuck in is the dark.

Most people can't tell the difference between them, the shadow and the dark. That's why you need me. Even if you don't know it. Or want to admit it. It's better you don't, in any case. Ignorance has a way of hiding, of obscuring the truth, creating blind spots. That's where I stalk, in the blind spots. And trust me when I tell you, you don't want to see the things I hunt, when the twilight settles in and the world is swallowed whole in one giant lightless bite. That's when you need me the most. When I come to life to save yours.

Even if you never see to thank me.

I knew I was in trouble even before my shadow trawler, Aurora Lux, stopped dead in her tracks on the Devil's Underpass. I'd been listening to the grinding cogs for kilometres, praying it was my hearing and not the accelerated leveraged gear shaft that gave her the distinct lumbering motion, something akin to a giant drunk baby, that set her apart from other land trawlers of her size.

She was a beast of a machine, globe-shaped and made almost entirely of Stygian glass, clamped together with ribbons of rough, soldered lead and giant rivets of brass. She sat high on the landscape, a whole working world beneath her in black steel and burnished copper, endless metres of greasy shafts and rusted cogs, polished clockwork wheels and ratcheted gears, like metal malformed intestines in the gut of a strange and wild beast, driven entirely by hissing steam and the wonders of Victorian engineering.

The Devil's Underpass was as bleak as its name. It was a slash on the earth, raw and red, as if the gods had slit the throat, but the zombie body of the monster landscape had refused to die. It was a throughfare, a no-man's land, with an escarpment that tunnelled it like the crest of a bloody wave made entirely of frozen rock. Aurora Lux's legs buckled and reset as she came to a blunt halt near the scarp face, her hydraulics driving her knees to a ninety degree angle to the foul drought-ridden earth beneath her square iron feet, as if she was squatting to take a robotic dump.

While she was moving I had light and was untouchable. While she was stopped, I was trapped in a cold ball of blackness, swamped by whatever surrounded me, a bull's-eye target at the mercy of whatever was out there and could climb. And that couldn't be good. I had to get her working again, even though the thought of descending into her gloomy, sooty bowels set my teeth on edge. It wasn't the waiting dark I was afraid of; it was what might be hiding in it. There was every chance I'd run into something I wasn't expecting by the time I worked my way down into the blinded core of her.

I watched until the last green pulse of her instruments died and the ghoulish reflection bled from my face. I already had the glow-worm extension lights on my bomber hat switched to high and their beams cut the dark like sheet lightning. I wasn't a fan of the strap, but I tucked my blonde curls high under the leather and buckled it tightly under my chin nevertheless, making sure my aviator cap wouldn't fall as I climbed down the clammy ladders. I pulled my goggles in place, flicking the levers to night-mode and watched as the world bled red. A fitting metaphor, I thought dismally, all things considered, for I suspected it wouldn't be long before my landscape bled for real. I could only pray it wouldn't be my blood that stained it when it finally flowed.

I could see my breath cut the light-beams and even though I was shivering, I slipped off my calf-length black pony overcoat, tightening the strings of my silk bustier until I felt the whalebone pinch and tucking the excess into the back of my leggings so nothing would get in the way at the wrong moment. My shadow cannon was already packed over my shoulder and I checked the blunt brass end to make sure it was clear to fire, before spiriting a thin horn-handled blade I called Clara inside the top of my thigh-high boot leathers. My air-pistols were already shoulder-holstered beneath a thick coiled fisherman's rope that cut my chest and to be careful not to weight myself too heavily, I tucked a tiny, pearl-handled revolver into the waistband of my moleskins.

I was as prepared as I would ever be.

I clicked on my ankle lights, opened the hatch and began to climb down.

The descent was brutal; ten flights of ladders, each one with barely a few inches of rest-space between and each pause leading to a more slippery ladder beneath, all cased within metal shafts so tight I had to be careful not to get permanently stuck. By the time I reached the half-way mark I was out of breath, the cold and claustrophobia sucking the oxygen straight from my lungs. I'd never make it down at this rate, let alone fight whatever I needed to. I gritted my teeth and spread my legs, gripping the outside of the ladder with my thighs and let go. I slid down the remaining flights like a firefighter sliding down a pole, landing hard on the steel-plated floor, despite my bent knees.

I smelled it before I saw it - and it was human. There was no mistaking the stench of that greasy, burnt flesh. I swallowed the swell of nausea and spat out a glob of mucus, revolving my shadow cannon over my shoulder to sweep the boiler room and swiftly drew an air-pistol from its strap.

It was a scene of carnage in spotlight.

Bloodied meat and ground tendons caught in gears, skin stretched over wheels, blood sticking in the cogs. It would take a gas-clamp to wrench that mangled femur from the gear shaft. No wonder Aurora Lux had died. Seemed I'd picked up a stowaway at my last stop at Giants' Bridge, but it wasn't the owner of the femur that made the hair on the back of my neck stand on end.

I spun anticlockwise as the grotesque beast struck from the shadows with a teeth-shattering screech, ripping the cap and goggles clean from my head. I closed my eyes. If it was anticipating an advantage in the aphotic cavern it was short-lived. My other senses had developed keener than eyes in shadow and I cartwheeled away from its foul breath, loosening the air-pistol into the void and slashing the creature's leg in a deep arc on my way around. It squealed like a wounded fox trying to claim the nightscape from a predator, but before I could sink another bullet into its oily chest, thirteen filthy claws snagged my rope and hoisted me hard against the mainsbridge. I fell violently onto my shadow cannon, crushing the handcut brass beneath me, knocking the air from my lungs and the air-pistol from my hand. It wasted no time, lunging what I imagined was a crude Acheronian dagger at my chest, but I rolled swiftly onto my side, releasing a bullet from my revolver into the stump of its ear as I desperately fought to get to my feet. My scrambling leathers found no grip on the bloodied floor and I slipped, tangling in my own rope as my head hit the steel-plated floor. It was then I felt thirteen clammy fingers rake the pulse in my neck.

They say when you're about to die you see your whole life played out, compressed into your last few precious seconds of breath. Seems I was about to find out. I felt the tip of blade press against throat flesh and the stab of adrenalin sliced my heart.

"What do you see?" I snarled as I opened my eyes and the blade tipped with blood.

"Nothing," it hissed, its dead eyes locked onto mine.

"That's why you have to die," I stared into that endless black abyss. "And nothing will miss you."

Much to its surprise, Clara's steel slid across the foul creature's throat like an ice-skater's blade on a slippery frozen rink. It dropped dead, despite already being dead, but as I pushed the putrid carcass to the floor I kicked my boot into the swampy flesh of its side, just in case. Its body would feed the furnace tonight as soon as I broke a bone from her gear shaft and got Aurora Lux up and running again.

Soon dawn will be here and I'll watch from my eyrie as the blazing sun cuts its golden teeth on the bleak horizon. The light will spill into every shadowed corner and we'll collectively sigh for the new day we made from the dark terrors of the night before.

But for now, tuck yourself in. Shut your eyes tight. Don't open them, whatever you do. Even when you feel the breath across the back of your neck. Convince yourself it's only childish fears you've outgrown. There's nothing really there.

But there's a reason children are afraid of the dark.

I am a child of the Cimmerian, bound to the edges of the crepuscular world where the eyes of men have closed. Do not be afraid if you see me.

Be afraid if you don't.

When the Night Bus Comes
David Turnbull

"When the night bus comes for you," said Chuck's grandfather, "you'll know before it even pulls up at your door."

For a decade the bus had been the subject of endless conversations between Chuck and his grandfather. On his twelfth birthday his father and grandfather had taken him fishing and revealed what was expected of him. It felt to Chuck as if he'd been in a state of anxiety and consternation ever since.

"How?" asked Chuck, rolling a smoke between his thumb and forefinger. "How will I know?"

His grandfather was sitting on a pile of motorcycle tires. "Gut feeling," he said. "A mixture of dread and elation. The bus has a weird aura that pulses ahead of it. Hits so hard it might bring you to your knees."

A knot tightened in Chuck's stomach. The way it always did whenever they spoke about the bus. "Do I really have to go?"

His grandfather reached over to where Chuck was sitting, put his boney hands on Chuck's shoulders and looked straight into his eyes. "Of course you do. It;s your duty. I done it. Your father done it. And my father before me. And my granddaddy. He was the first."

Chuck screwed up his face. "That old bastard was the one that cursed us."

"Cursed us and blessed us," said his grandfather. "A dozen of one. A dozen of the other."

"It's because of him I have to go on the bus," Chuck pointed out.

Chuck's grandfather pushed his long hair back behind his ears.

Chuck had an unspoken sense of pride that his grandfather didn't fit the image most people have of a man in his mid-seventies. He wasn't a grey haired old soul in a knitted cardigan and carpet slippers. He'd been a metal head since he discovered Led Zeppelin in his twenties. Ever true to the image he'd cultivated back then, he kept his hair long and dyed it jet black. He was always dressed in a battered leather jacket, tee shirt and faded blue jeans. He had a bit of hooked nose and at a certain angle he looked a lot like Alice Cooper without the mascara. He rode a Harley and ran a repair shop for vintage motorcycles.

"It's because of my old granddaddy that nothing really bad ever happens in this family," his grandfather said.

"Except the bus,' Chuck shot back.

This was an old argument. The two of them had been back and forth on it dozens of times. Never seen eye to eye. Chuck's grandfather sighed, wiped some axle grease from his hands with a rag and picked up a spanner. "Some of us have got work to do," he said and switched on his beat up old CD player. A Black Sabbath track echoed at full blast through the workshop, effectively bringing the conversation to an end.

***

Chuck went straight round to see Shelly. Shelly was his lady. They'd been together since High School. She was the only girl in his carpentry class. Shelly was cool. They were solid. Most High School romances don't last the course but, because of the bus, nothing bad ever happened in Chuck's family. So nothing bad had ever befallen their relationship.

They drank some beer, ordered a pizza and made out on her couch. In the aftermath, when Chuck was sitting with his arm around her and her head was nuzzling on his chest he finally plucked up the courage to bring up the matter of his potentially imminent departure.

"Babe, there's going to come a time when I have to go away for a while."

She unraveled herself from his embrace and sat up straight, red hair mussed up from their passionate tussle. "Away?"

"A family thing I can't get out of."

"Where's away? How far away?"

Chuck drew a deep breath. "Quite far."

"When, Chuck?

"That's not settled yet,' he said. "Could be soon. Could be some time."

Shelly took his face in her hands and turned his head toward her. Her green eyes had tears welling up in them. "Are you planning on breaking up with me?"

"No, no, babe," Chuck assured her. "Nothing like that." He leaned forward to kiss her. She pushed him away, face flushing angrily. "You better be straight with me right now, Charles Deakin. We swore there would be no secrets between us."

This wasn't going well. Shelly only ever used his full, proper name when she was pretty damned pissed with him. "Fair enough," he said. "I'm going to give it to you straight. But don't blame me if you find what I'm about to tell you impossible to believe."

Shelly looked angrier than ever. She moved to the armchair, folded her arms stiffly and stared moodily over at him. "Go on then, I'm all ears."

So Chuck told her the story. The one that had been in his family for generations.

He told her about William Deakin, also known as Willie, or Fly Willie to some.

His grandfather's grandfather.

How he was a truck driver back in the 1930's, just before the war, delivering eggs and butter and jars of pickle to general stores in little off the beaten track towns and hamlets. And how he wasn't such a good driver and how, without the benefit of modern day satnav, he often got lost on country roads that back then were little more than dirt tracks that could lead you round in a complex labyrinth of intersecting circuits.

And how one night he got so frustrated at going round in circles that he cracked open a jar of moonshine he'd bought from a shopkeeper who ran a still from his outhouse. And how he was slugging it as he drove and cursing his luck as the moon rose and the night grew darker.

And how a young couple only two weeks married came hurtling around a corner in a boneshaker of an old model T Ford they'd bought for song from a gas station proprietor. And how their brakes were shot to pieces. And how Fly Willie, inebriated from the moonshine, didn't see them till it was way too late.

Shelly was watching him with an exasperated expression.

"What's any of this got to do with you going away?"

"I'm coming to that, babe," said Chuck. He picked up one of the beer cans and tipped back his neck so he could wet his mouth with the dregs. Then he carried on.

"Fly Willie's truck fared a lot better than the Model T. The truck's engine had crumpled back on itself like a concertina but it took all of the impact and the truck was still upright. The radiator hissed like a kettle on the boil and swirled steam all over the road. Willie had a gash on his head from where it hit the steering wheel. But other than a bit of disorientation he was ok."

Chuck reached for one of the other beer cans and shook its meagre contents into his mouth. "The Model T on the other hand was knocked clean off the road. It rolled down into a gully and was lying on its back, wheels still spinning. Willie scrambled down into the gully. The couple were in a bad way. Faces all bloodied, necks twisted at such horrible angles that Willie was in no doubt that they were both busted. Willie checked their pulses. Their wrists were already cold and lifeless.

Willie started to panic. He could lose his job over this. He'd got wife at home and a kid on the way."

Chuck looked up at Shelly.

"His son was my grandfather's father."

"I could have figured that out," said Shelly.

"Anyway, he crawled on his hands and knees out of the gully and back up to the road. All the time he looked around for the lights from a farmhouse where he might go and get help. It was full dark by then and he couldn't see a thing. There was nothing but crickets chirruping and the steady hiss of the steam from the radiator. He tried the engine but it's futile. He paced up and down on the road, completely at a loss as to what he could to do next. Then he saw it coming out of the darkness."

Shelly leaned forward, fully attentive now.

"What, Chuck? What does he see?"

"Maybe it's the headlights of another car. But they looked weird. They we're kind of glassy and silvery. Like the way the eyes of a cat reflects back the light from the moon. And there was a noise drawing closer. A terrible growling noise that vibrated up through the ground. And Willie wondered if it was a combination of the hooch and a concussion giving him hallucinations.

"And then it emerged from the shadows and it was not at all what Willie imagined."

"What, Chuck?" repeated Shelly. "What was it?"

"A bus."

"A bus?"

Chuck nodded.

"But not like any bus Fly Willie had ever seen in his life before. It was long and slick. It seemed to move by stretching and contracting, rather than rolling on wheels. Its chassis didn't look rigid. It curved flaccidly as it took the bend. When it glided to a halt, Willie pressed his hand against its side. It felt warm and leathery. Willie thought he could feel the throb of a pulse."

"So it was an animal," said Shelly. "Not a bus at all. An animal."

"It looked like a bus," said Chuck. "It had the appearance of a bus. Flat sections that look like windows, but are black as the rest of it. Circular objects jutting from its belly that looked like wheels with dark, hoary hubcaps. And a door that hissed open like a serpent stretching its jaw."

Shelly's green eyes went wide. "Was there a driver inside?"

"Willie couldn't be sure. It looked like a driver but all he could see was a shape within a silhouette. Maybe it was an extension of the bus itself. A kind of facsimile of a driver."

Chuck shook another beer can to see if there was anything left in the bottom to wet his mouth. He tipped it up and licked his lips. "And a voice came from the bus."

Shelly edged forward another inch in the armchair. "The driver?"

"It seemed so," said Chuck. "But Willie couldn't tell for sure.

All of this can go away, it said. *It can be made to seem as if you were never here. That those unfortunate souls just skidded and went off the road by accident."*

Willie looked down into the gully at the smoking wreck. The wheels had stopped spinning. The night was silent. In the ominous presence of the strange bus even the crickets had stopped chirruping.

How, asked Willie. *How can this all go away?*

Step inside, came the reply. *Ride the night bus and no blame will attach itself to you."*

"If I had been Willie," said Shelly, "I'd have ran from there as fast as my legs would carry me."

"But Willie didn't run," said Chuck. "He asked how far and for how long he has to ride the bus to make it all go away."

"I know how these things go," said Shelly. "It's for eternity. The bus, or whatever it is, wants Willie's soul."

Chuck shook his head. "I wish that was so. But the voice in the bus said - *You have to ride for as far and as long as it takes.* And Willie asked for as far and as long as it takes for what? And the voice on the bus says – *as long as it takes for them to feed and be satisfied."*

Shelly moved back to the sofa. "Them?"

Chuck nodded. "It turned out that there are things inside the bus. Things that dwell in the shadows. They're like parasites. They feed on human fears. And to make it all go away Fly Willie had to agree to be scared witless so they could have their supper."

"I would definitely have run for my life at that point," said Shelly. "But I bet Willie got on the bus."

"He did," said Chuck. "But first he had to agree to the fare."

Shelly creased her brow. "Hang on, I thought he had to feed the things in the shadows."

"That was the cost of making the car crash go away," said Chuck. "But the fare for riding the bus was that the first born son of every generation of Willie's family from that moment on had to take a ride on the night bus and feed the things in the shadows."

"And that's why you have to go?" asked Shelly. "Because you're the first born of your generation?"

Chuck nodded solemnly. "Yep."

Shelly fell silent.

Chuck watched her, feeling his shoulders tense from trepidation. Finally she turned to him and shook her head. "I'm not buying this."

Chuck sighed. "I knew you wouldn't believe me."

"Oh, I believe you, Chuck," she said. "We've known each other since we were fourteen and you've never once lied to me. Leastways not that I'm aware of."

Chuck shuffled closer to her. "So what is it you're not buying, babe?"

"The deal," she replied. "The whole first born son has to pay the fare thing."

"That's just the way it is," said Chuck, feeling he was sounding a bit like his grandfather.

"It doesn't make any sense," she said. "You guys are no better off than anyone else. Your grandfather mends motorcycles. Your folks live in that big, fancy house up on the hill. But your dad's the chauffeur and your mum's the housekeeper. You work as a vending machine operative. Good things are not exactly happening in your life."

Chuck reached out and stroked her hair. "Babe, you're not understanding. Paying the fare doesn't make good things happen. It prevents bad things from happening."

Shelly's face turned pink. "Don't you patronize me, Charles Deakin."

And that was when the argument kicked off. And it was bad. Really bad. And all the way through it Chuck was thinking- *why is this happening? Bad stuff is not supposed to happen.*

***

Usually when he went to Shelly's he ended up spending the night but not this time. The argument was way too intense, too many insults were hurled in words of thoughtless anger. Instead he went home and laid on the bed, going back over it, blow by blow. When eventually he drifted into sleep he dreamed, as he always did, of the bus.

It came for him, sleek and slithering, stretching back for miles and miles along an open highway. When the doors hissed open he stepped through its waiting jaws and into its belly. The seats were filled with passengers. And each one had been decapitated.

Their raw, ragged necks gurgled blood and were hung with gruesome garlands of sinew. Their heads sat on their laps. As he passed along the aisle that seem to stretch toward infinity, the heads turned to him and said in unison.

"It's worse than you imagine. Far, far worse than you imagine."

And he saw them in the darkness. The ancient, squirming, tentacled things that waited to engorge themselves on his terror. The heads laughed and mocked him. The laughter rose to a maniacal crescendo. So loud he snapped awake in a cold trembling sweat.

***

"Shelly says she'll walk if I go on the bus."

His grandfather set the exhaust pipe he'd been cleaning down on his workbench. He had his hair tied back in a ponytail and was wearing a black Judas Priest tee-shirt, revealing the sleeves of multiple tattoos that adorned his wrinkled arms.

"You told her?"

"We don't have secrets," said Chuck.

"Well, you damn well should," said his grandfather. "Especially when it comes to the bus. The bus is something only we menfolk should ever discuss."

"We menfolk?" said Chuck. 'That sounds like a hangover from Fast Willie's days. It's pretty damn misogynistic."

His grandfather shook his head. "And that sounds like something that came out of Shelly's mouth, not yours."

"That's beside the point," said Chuck. "Nothing bad is supposed to happen. But we had a huge bust up. If I go on the bus she'll walk for good."

His grandfather scooped up a handful of scattered bolts and dropped them into a plastic container "And how bad do you think it'll get if you don't go on the bus?"

Chuck threw up his arms. "Who knows? Maybe this whole thing is just a steaming crock of shit."

"I know you know that not true," said his grandfather.

"You do, do you?" asked Chuck, feeling uncharacteristically belligerent. "What makes you so sure?"

"It's in your blood, son. Ever since Fly Willie first set foot on that bus it's ran in the blood of our family."

"Maybe I'll be the one to end this," said Chuck. "Maybe when that godforsaken bus rolls up I'll just turn around and walk away."

"Do that and there would be dire consequences," his grandfather warned. "If you break the pact there's generations of bad luck held behind that particular beaver damn. Once it's breached there will be no holding back. We'll all get washed away in a deluge of bad shit."

Chuck gave a shrug of his shoulders. "What's the worst that can happen?"

"I could get cancer," said his grandfather. "Your father could go over a ravine in that limo he drives for his boss. Your mum could fall down the marble stairs in that big house. You could get electrocuted by faulty wiring in one of those vending machines. The possibilities for bad shit are endless, Chuck. Endless and pretty relentless. Just look at the tragedies other families endure. You want something to happen to Shelly?"

"On the other hand I could lose her altogether," Chuck pointed out.

"I don't know why you had to tell her."

"I couldn't just disappear without explanation when the bus comes."

"She'd never know," said his grandfather.

"Of course she would," insisted Chuck. "I could be gone for days, months even, according to what you told me."

"Time inside the bus is as weird as the bus looks on the outside," said his grandfather. "What seems like days and months inside might only be a few minutes on the outside. That's how Fast Willie was able to report his truck as stolen and how he was never connected to the death of the couple."

"So If I went on the bus Shelly would never even know I was gone?"

His grandfather nodded.

"How come I never knew this?"

"It was your father's job to tell you."

Chuck clicked his tongue against the roof of his mouth. "He never gave me any specifics, other than to confirm that everything you told me was true. Any time I tried to ask him anything he'd just turn away and say it was too traumatic to talk about."

Chuck's grandfather rolled his eyes. "Your father was always a bit of a disappointment to me."

"I guess I'd be a worse disappointment if I didn't go on the bus?" said Chuck.

"Well now, you know that Shelly need never know, it should make your decision a whole lot easier. You have to man up, Chuck. For all our sakes. And now…"

"I know," said Chuck. "Some of us have got work to do."

His grandfather pressed play on his CD player. The track today was AC/DC *Highway to Hell,* which Chuck felt was ironically appropriate in the circumstances.

***

Chuck was replenishing one of the vending machines at the mall when he saw Shelly had gone for lunch in the cafeteria area. Shelly worked as a supervisor at a frozen yoghurt concession. She was with one of her colleagues, both in the pale blue polo shirt and matching cap that formed the concession's uniform.

Her colleague was a guy, broad shouldered and tanned, Hispanic looking. They were chatting in an animated manner, laughing loudly. The way Shelly was looking over the table at him, head slightly cocked to one side, had more than a hint of flirtation about it.

Chuck felt wounded. A deep pang of jealousy gnawed at him. Any other time he might have marched over and confronted her. But he restrained himself, knowing that the dumbest thing he could do was make a bad situation worse.

He finished off his job, locked the vending machine and carried out the necessary tests to make sure everything was in working order. He heard Shelly laugh and bit down nervously on his lip. Without looking back he hurried out of the mall and down to the basement parking level to pick up his wagon.

Once he'd loaded his gear and checked his inventory he sent Shelly a text message on his cellphone. *Hi babe. How's your day? Miss you.* He waited a good five minutes before setting off. A reply didn't come.

***

According to the story the bus devoured Fly Willie's mangled truck.

The way his grandfather told it the bus ploughed right over the wreck. And Fly Willie heard the truck and the trailer and the engine being crunched and chewed up and swallowed. Not a nut or bolt was left in the dirt. Not so much as the tiniest drop of oil or the hint of a skid mark from the tires was left. The truck was gone. And with it any evidence that Fly Willie had ever been on that stretch of road.

And when he had endured what he had to endure for as long as it took to satisfy the creatures inside the bus, he was set down in the town from which he'd started when he became lost. And it was like he had hardly been gone at all. And he walked into the sheriff's office and reported his track stolen.

That part of the story made complete sense to Chuck now.

He'd always wondered why Willie's wife hadn't reported him missing.

A few weeks later a young reporter had tracked down the filling station owner who'd sold the young couple the model T Ford. He'd been so full of remorse and guilt at having made a fateful fast buck from selling a vehicle with faulty brakes that he hung himself from the rafters of his garage, giving the young reporter another scoop.

No one had ever connected Fly Willie's stolen truck to the tragic events on the country road. It was so long gone now that no one ever would. But the filling station owner had paid the price. Chuck often wondered if sometimes the bad stuff meant for his family leaked its way through that beaver damn and just flowed to the nearest convenient conduit.

Chuck also often wondered, as he did now, lying on his bed, if there were other families with a distant relative who'd been enticed onto the bus and had been burdened with the generational debt that the fare perpetually generated. Was there another Chuck in another town somewhere, worrying and fretting about how he would react when the bus pulled up? Wrestling with the pros and cons of what might be right or wrong in this situation?

When he eventually slipped into sleep, his dream of the bus was inevitable and predictable. *"It's worse than you imagine. Far, far worse than you imagine,"* said the severed heads of the headless passengers that mocked him in a crescendo of maniacal laughter.

***

Chuck snapped awake with the absolute certainty that the bus was approaching. It was exactly as his grandfather had suggested. He was seized by an overwhelming sense of dread. But at the same time his nerve ends tingled with adrenalin charged excitement. The little hairs on his arms stood on end. Sweat sprouted on his brow like a viral rash.

Trembling and breathing rapidly, he rose from the bed. His legs felt as if they could hardly hold his weight as he cautiously pulled his curtains slightly to one side. And here it came, sleek beneath the moonlight, so fat it filled the entire street, as dark in hue as the oil in the bowels of the Earth.

If any of his neighbors looked out they wouldn't register it. It was apparently invisible to anyone but its intended passenger. His grandfather had told him that was how these things worked. It had come for him straight out of baseball practice one October night and none of his teammates so much as blinked at its presence.

Now the bus rippled forward and hushed to a halt by the front entrance to his apartment block. *I could turn my back*, thought Chuck, *I could simply refuse to climb on board*. His grandfather's words came back to berate him. *I could get cancer. Your father could go over a ravine in that limo he drives for his boss. Your mum could fall down the marble stairs in that big house. You could get electrocuted by faulty wiring in one of those vending machines. The possibilities for bad shit are endless, Chuck.*

Did he want all that on his head?

Did he want to risk some tragedy befalling Shelly?

The time for procrastination was over.

The bus was here, waiting for him to board.

There was no choice. He had an obligation. He to keep his side of Fly Willie's bargain. Feeling sick to the stomach, heart palpitating, he pulled on whatever clothes were to hand. His bedside clock showed that it was 2:40 in the morning. He didn't think it would matter one iota to the bus or the dark things that festered in its belly whether he washed and shaved before boarding.

He looked around his apartment before leaving. It could be weeks or even months before he was back here. But in real time he'd be gone no longer than the time it took to fetch a glass of water from the kitchen. Shelly would wake in the morning none the wiser to the fact that he'd acted against her wishes. They would kiss and make up. Nothing bad would ever happen and she would never know why.

And if they had a son?

He'd cross that bridge when he came to it.

One day at a time, as the old saying went.

He closed the door behind him and went slowly down the stairs like a condemned man taking his last walk. When he opened the door the bus was there, waiting in all its monstrous malevolence.

He saw the flat sections that looked like windows, but were as black as the rest of it. He saw the circular objects jutting from its belly that looked like wheels with dark, hoary hubcaps. Vapor rose in dancing swirls from its obsidian hide. It seemed to throb rhythmically as if a heart pulsed tarry blood through the tangled veins of its wiring.

Tentatively he pressed the palm of his hand against the side, just as Fly Willie had done all those years ago. It wasn't rigid, as the side of a bus should be. It didn't feel metallic. Rather it felt smooth and supple. The way he imagined an eel might feel to the touch.

He was suddenly filled with a sense of how ageless an entity it was. He thought of how it may have evolved and transformed through different stages of human history, adapting to its environment. It had taken the form of a bus in the twentieth century and still remained true to that form. But who knew what metamorphosis waited in centuries to come? Who knew what appearance it had taken in the past?

The bus purred and juddered. The doors hissed open. He felt like a rabbit frozen in the path of a venomous snake about to strike. Inside he saw the shadowy appendage that had been formed in the shape of the driver. A grotesquerie with no purpose other than the mimicry of reality.

"*Step inside,*" implored a seductive, disembodied voice that seemed at one and the same time to be in Chuck's head as well as emanating from the interior of the bus

Like a flash of light Chuck had a moment of absolute clarity. He knew what he had to do. It was in his gift to end this once and for all. At least for his family. He could make the ultimate sacrifice and simply not ever get back with Shelly. He could self-condemn himself to a solitary and celibate lifestyle. That way he'd have kept the bargain, but there would be no risk of another first born son to shoulder the burden of the Fast Willie's fare.

He stepped onto the bus and wondered if he had the strength of character to stick by that. Or whether what he was about to endure would be so bad he wouldn't be able to stop himself from running to the comfort of Shelly's arms as soon as he stepped back off.

The air inside was clammy and musky. It made him gag. The doors hissed shut behind him. The engine growled and the bus juddered. He felt his stomach turn as the bus glided from the sidewalk.

He reached for something to steady himself. What he touched felt wet and tremulous. His hand recoiled in terrified repulsion. Apprehensively he peered into the darkness of the long, narrow aisle ahead of him. At first, he could see nothing at all. Then as his eyes grew accustomed to the darkness, he began to discern vague shapes and jittery movements within the shapes.

And what gradually materialized before him was worse than he had ever imagined.

Far, far worse.

The Price of Ignorance
Wondra Vanian

Freya didn't know she was destined to be a witch when she woke the morning of the equinox. She didn't even know what an equinox *was*. If she had known about the hidden world of witches and what the equinox meant to young witches like her, she might have done things a bit differently.

That was what she told herself, anyway.

The Autumn Equinox fell on a Friday that year. Freya got up—late, as usual—and made ready for school without realizing it was a special day to millions of witches around the world. To her, it was just another day. The only thing special about that Friday for Freya was the dance at the high school, following the football game.

She never made it to the dance.

reya spent so long trying to decide between the blue sweater and the yellow cardigan she was already five minutes late when she hurried out the front door. The fact that her mother refused to give her a ride made her even more irritable. Like her job came before her only child?

Well, if Freya got detention for being late again—which she undoubtedly would—her mother would have to sort it out. It was *her* fault, after all.

Freya stopped dead at the end of her driveway.

"What. The. Hell?"

There, staring at her from across the road, was a large red fox. She didn't even know they *had* those in her state. Weren't they supposed to be dangerous?

"Uh…" she said uncertainly, "shoo?"

The fox tilted its head to the side, as if weighing her words. He (she was *so* not checking out its junk, eww) completely ignored her.

Yup, definitely a he.

Freya looked around for something to throw and found nothing but the pebbles that lined the driveway. She grabbed one of the larger ones and threw it. It fell several feet short. The fox just twitched his tail.

A car rolled up, cutting off Freya's view of the insolent beast.

"Hey, Freya! You late too?"

Clarke, running back for the varsity team, leaned across the car, smiling up at her through the open window. She smiled back, glad she'd spent the time plumping her lips.

"Yeah. My mom's being a total bitch and won't give me a ride."

Rolling his eyes as if to say, "Parents, right?" Clarke popped the door open. "Hop in." She was way too excited to be riding in an upperclassman's car to check to see if the fox was still watching.

Freya forgot all about the fox until they'd parked and were climbing out of Clarke's car.

"Huh," he said, bemused. "Would'ya look at that?" He pointed across the parking lot to a large fox watching them. Freya shuddered.

"What's the point of having custodians if they let vermin run riot?" She awrinkled her nose in distaste, glad she sounded more annoyed and less freaked the crap out. Had that thing *followed them*?

Clarke grinned. "Don't worry; I'll take care of it." He ducked into the car, rummaged in the glovebox and came back with a pistol.

Freya instinctively took a step back when she saw the gun. Clarke had always seemed so with it, so cool... but, bringing a gun to school? Dick move.

He pointed the gun at the fox.

"No, wait." The animal made Freya uneasy and it was weirder than hell that it had followed her all the way to school, but that didn't mean she wanted it to *die*. It was just some dumb animal. Besides, if the school guards heard a gunshot and found her there…

Ugh. Freya did *not* need that kind of hassle. She'd be grounded until the end of time.

"You said it yourself," Clarke said, taking aim, "it's just vermin..."

The fox looked directly at Freya, met her eye and tilted its head, as if silently pleading for her help. She didn't know why, but she couldn't let him kill it. It wasn't even the gun thing, it was just… wrong. Freya laid a hand on Clarke's arm.

"If you shoot that thing, we'll both get expelled."

At first, Freya thought he'd do it anyway. Clarke shrugged and let his arm drop.

"You're right. My dad would lose his shit if I got arrested for shooting at some stupid animal."

Freya relaxed as Clarke reached into the car to return the gun to its hiding spot. When she glanced at the spot where the fox had been, it was empty. Weird.

Clarke threw his arm around Freya, leading her toward the school. "If anyone asks, we're late because I had to rescue you from a rabid animal."

It was hard not to think about the fox's odd behavior as word of Clarke's heroic rescue spread through the school. By the end of the day, Freya's staring fox had turned into a savage beast that had all but ripped her face off by the time Clarke had come to her rescue.

"I'm glad you're okay," a freshman told her after last bell. "You were so lucky Clarke was there." The girl's eyes went all misty. "I'd *kill* to be rescued by him."

"Yeah," Freya said absently, "sure. Gotta go." She'd taken only a few steps out the front doors of the building when a familiar sports car roared up.

"Heya Freya!" Clarke leaned across a pretty blonde Freya recognized as a varsity cheerleader. "We're grabbing a bite before the game. You comin'?"

Freya hesitated. Her mother had been insistent that Freya come home right after school. But her mother had also forced her to find her own way there... If she hadn't, Freya wouldn't have gotten a ride from Clarke and the whole school wouldn't be talking about her.

Screw it.

"Yeah." She climbed into the back seat, squished in with two other members of the football team. They kept up a steady stream of inane chatter as they sped through the town toward the burger joint where kids normally hung out after school.

Freya's phone went off three times while they ate. She assumed the angry buzzing came from her mother, so she ignored it. When she made a trip to the bathroom, she took the opportunity to check her messages.

Where are you?
I told you to come straight home.
Freya! Call me NOW.

Freya rolled her eyes at the phone.

Going to the game, she texted back. *Be home late.*

Then she turned her phone off. She'd get hell for it later, but she was mad enough at her mother not to care.

The others had to get back to the high school to prepare for the game. Clarke offered to give Freya a ride home first, but she just shook her head. "Naw," she said, "I'll just hang around 'til kickoff."

Freya, Clarke, and the others piled into the car and headed back to school—or, started to, at least. Before they even made it out of the parking lot, the cheerleader squealed. "Look, a fox! I bet it's the rabid one that attacked Freya!"

Freya's heart pounded. The fox again. How did it keep finding her? Why was it following her? Was that normal behavior for a fox? She'd never seen a fox in her *life* and now she had her very own fox stalker. It didn't make sense.

"Yeah, man," one of Clarke's teammates said, "get that thing!"

No.

Something about running down a poor, defenseless animal seemed terribly wrong. It was more than that, though. Something about killing *that* fox seemed so much worse.

"Don't" she said, but the boys were cheering Clarke on and the other girl was shrieking and they were wheeling toward the fox...

Thu-ump.

Freya's stomach did a sickening flop. Her head swam and she went cold all over.

No.

It wasn't really doing anything wrong...

The others congratulated Clarke in whoops and fist bumps. Freya couldn't bring herself to join in. She sat in a numb daze all the way back to the school. No one else seemed to notice her somber mood as they parked and climbed out of the car.

"See ya later!" Clarke called as he and the others made their ways to the locker rooms. Freya didn't bother replying; their attention had already turned to the upcoming game, anyway.

Freya needed to sit down. She felt like she might be sick. There were benches outside the offices. She started toward them...

Only to be brought up short when something caught her from behind. She tried to scream but a thick cloth was pressed against her face. Freya only realized the rag must have been soaked in some sort of drug when the world went fuzzy. She blacked out.

Freya lost consciousness in the high school parking lot. She came to deep in a forest—not that she knew that right away; there was a dark, heavy hood over her head. It was made of some thick material that made breathing difficult. She tried to remove it but found her hands held firmly behind her back.

Panic tried to take her. God, what was *happening*?

The hands holding her pushed Freya forward. She heard whispered voices as a deep, rich voice commanded her to "Walk." Her step was unsteady on the uneven ground. Hands caught her when something snagged her foot. They weren't kind, but they kept Freya from falling on her face, so she was grateful for them.

"Stop."

She did as she was told. What else could she do?

Another voice spoke. "Who challenges her?" Freya didn't recognize the voice—but she *did* recognize the next one.

"I do."

"*Mom?*" Tears stung Freya's eyes. What did her mom have to do with this? Was she being punished for being tardy? For ignoring her mother's texts? If so, it was a bit extreme. If it wasn't some kind of punishment, Freya couldn't even begin to imagine what was going on.

Her mother spoke again, ignoring Freya's question.

"Freya Morgan, you have been challenged." Something hard pressed against her throat. She jerked back but the hands holding her pushed her forward again. The thing at her throat bit, drawing blood.

Oh, God... is that a knife?

"If there is fear in your heart, it would be better to step forward into this blade than enter the circle. Is there fear in your heart?"

Was there fear in her heart? How could there *not* be fear in her heart? What kind of stupid question was that? She couldn't see; she didn't know where she was; her mother was holding a knife to her throat and she could hear people muttering. Of *course* she was afraid!

Don't be stupid, Freya told herself. *It's your mom. She's not actually going to hurt you. This is the woman who kissed your skinned knees and taught you how to use tampons. She's not going to stab you in front of an audience, no matter how many texts you ignore.*

Peace settled over Freya. She relaxed.

"Is there fear in your heart?"

Freya started to shake her head then remembered the knife. "I'm not afraid," she said.

"Then step forward."

Step forward? Onto the knife? Was she nuts?

But Freya knew her mother wouldn't ask her to do anything that was truly dangerous. She stepped forward...

And felt a cool rush of night air as the hood was removed. She took several deep, grateful breaths before she looked around at the people watching her.

Freya stood in the center of an enormous circle of people and candles. Huge trees rose up all around them. Her eyes grew wide as she took in their odd surroundings. Finally, her gaze fell on the women in front of her. One was her mother. The other was...

"Aunt Michelle?" Freya asked, astonished. Her mother's best friend.

The other woman nodded, eyes twinkling. She made a gesture with her hand and the person holding Freya released her. Freya didn't immediately rush to her mother's side. Something about the weird robes her mother wore made her uneasy.

"Freya Morgan, you have been challenged and you have been tested. To take your rightful place in our circle, all that remains is to call forth your familiar and cement the bond that will make you the witch you were born to be."

Witch? Mom's a witch? That's... that's actually kind of cool.

"Familiar? What's that?"

It was Freya's mother that answered. "Your familiar will be an animal that has chosen you to be its master. You probably would have noticed it already. They tend to show themselves in the days before a witch's initiation."

Yellow eyes watching from across the road.

Oh, no.

A sinking feeling came over Freya. "What if, uh, what if I don't have a familiar?"

Aunt Michelle and her mother exchanged a look. "Every witch has a familiar," Aunt Michelle explained. "Without question."

"What if something happened to my familiar?"

"Something? Something like what, exactly?"

A murmur ran through the circle of robed people. Freya's stomach clenched painfully.

"Like, um, what if it died?"

The murmur became a loud grumble.

"Honey," her mother said, "did something happen?"

"Enough," Aunt Michelle said. The circle quieted. "To take your rightful place in the circle, you must call forth your familiar. Do it now, Freya." Fun Aunt Michelle was gone. This was business.

Freya knew that, if she tried, she would fail. But, what else could she do? Everyone was staring at her. So, she closed her eyes and thought of the fox that had been watching her all day. The fox whose mangled body probably still laid on the dirty concrete of the diner's parking lot. A gasp ran through the gathered witches, making Freya's eyes fly open —just as the ghostly image of a fox sauntered in to the circle.

"Oh, no," Freya's mother whispered.

The fox walked up to Aunt Michelle, sat on its haunches and looked up. Freya had the weird sensation that they were communicating somehow. Her suspicions were confirmed when Aunt Michelle's brows drew together in a frown.

"Freya? Did you... did you cause your familiar to come to harm?"

"It... it wasn't *really* my fault. I mean…"

The ghostly fox turned to stare accusingly at Freya. She hung her head.

Gasps of shock ran through the circle. Shame made Freya's face burn. She couldn't speak; all she could do was nod miserably.

"Freya, no." Tears dropped from her mother's eyes and landed on her cheeks. "Baby, no..."

Aunt Michelle laid a hand on her mother's arm. "I'm sorry," she said. Her voice was full of regret.

Freya was confused. Why was Aunt Michelle apologizing to her mother? It was Freya who'd screwed up, she should be the one apologizing.

"I'm sorry," Freya began, but Aunt Michelle held up a hand to silence her.

When Aunt Michelle spoke again, it was in a loud, authoritative voice that carried through the meadow. "There is one way to enter the circle and two ways out. You leave one with the elements as a daughter of the earth," her voice faltered but, swallowing hard, she continued, "or, the elements take you."

Elements take you? What did that even *mean*? They hadn't gotten to the Periodic Table yet... Freya looked to her mother for an explanation but the woman had her face buried in her hands.

"Freya Morgan," Aunt Michelle continued, "you have committed an unforgiveable crime. A familiar pledged its life to you and you returned its fidelity with violence. You owe your familiar a life."

"A... a life?"

It happened too quickly for Freya to see. Aunt Michelle lunged forward, blade glinting in the moonlight. Freya felt the warm blood spilling down her breast before she felt the searing pain in her throat. She felt to the ground, her mother's sobs unusually loud in the suddenly quiet field. As her blood seeped into the dirt, the ghostly figure of the dead fox sauntered over to Freya. As it had the first time she'd seen it, the fox sat and watched motionlessly as Freya paid the price for her ignorance.

Maggoty Jo
Diane Arrelle

Florida couldn't believe her eyes. Maggots: thousands maybe hundreds of thousands of them, covered the trash can. They turned the sides and the inside of the lid of her garbage can wriggling white. She'd just walked out to dump her daily bag of cat litter and was confronted with this.

"Holy shit!" She yelped and backed away from the parasites escaping the huge canister. They were dropping down from the edge of the lid like an oozing flood of slimy white lava.

She began to shake with revulsion, then turned and ran into the garage. She stared at the piles of stuff jammed onto shelves and scattered all over the cement floor and dug through it to find what she needed. Florida grasped a spray can of common insecticide and a gallon of super-strength, super-toxic, pest remover labeled too dangerous for use. "Thank goodness Ralph left this behind!"

She closed the garage door, then shut the warped, wooden back door to the house. She needed to be sure none of the dozen or so milling cats could get out through the torn and rusted screen door.

Florida took out the spray can and saturated the disgusting white carnivores feasting on her refuse. "Die!" she screamed, not caring if any of her neighbors heard her. Then she laughed and did a victory dance around the trashcan as the maggots writhed, poured up over the lip and plummeted down to the blacktop.

Her dancing stopped abruptly as they wriggled to get out of the sunlight and into the shade. None of them died but appeared to move as a unit toward the shade under the broken, webbed chairs on her driveway.

"Huh? Why aren't you suckers dying? I used almost the whole can on you."

The maggots ignored her as they sped across the hot asphalt.

"Well, I'll get you yet!" Florida bellowed and opened the container of toxic insecticide. She dumped half on the maggots fleeing the sunlight and dumped the rest of the incredibly potent smelling liquid into the can. She slammed the cover on it and watched the driveway horde writhe, but not expire.

She felt sweat forming on her forehead and upper lip. She'd had enough and went inside, stepped over the lounging cats and gently pushed the wandering ones out of her way as she headed for the kitchen and, after filling the teakettle, put it on a lit burner.

A few minutes later Florida filled a mug with boiling water. She dropped in a dried-up used teabag and then took the rest of the almost full pot outside and dumped it on the maggots, who were apparently unfazed by the chemicals she'd just used on them.

The scalding water poured over them and most stopped moving and died. The few that appeared to be immune to every torture continued to flee the light. She ignored them and kept the trashcan lid closed, hoping the insecticides would do their job. She grunted with satisfaction at the carnage at her feet and went inside for her cup of almost clear water. She decided she deserved a new teabag as a reward for vanquishing the filthy, germ carrying, carrion eaters.

A few hours later, the dead maggots crisping up in the sun, Florida finally opened the back door and let the cats wander in and out through the rusted torn screen-door. All was right in her world except that Jo, her ten-year-old calico, had disappeared two days earlier. Florida knew that older cats tended to wander off to die. Poor Jo had lost a lot of weight and her fur looked matted and dull. Florida had raised enough cats over the last thirty years to recognize a cat that was dying and even though ten years wasn't old, it was old for a sickly cat.

She walked outside, glanced down at the multitude of tiny white carcasses and grinned. "Chalk up one for the human." She licked her pointer finger and made an imaginary line in the air.

The next morning Florida opened the door and was greeted by what seemed to be dozens of flies. They were bigger than the average housefly and were buzzing like the incredibly discordant horn section of an orchestra. "Good lord," she shouted and grabbed the nearly empty bug spray. She sprayed the screen but the flies ignored the poisonous liquid so she shooed them away. They took off and she saw dozens more on the trash can. She ran over with a broom and shooed them away as well and then opened the lid.

A black swarm poured out and upward, settling on her arms and hair. She screamed, dropped the lid and, slapping at her head, ran into the house, slamming the door behind her.

She sat at the table, watching the cats eating from the unwashed dishes all around the kitchen. If one got near her she'd pet it for a moment. The day was hot and she kept the unscreened windows shut as well as the door. She wished she still had a working fan. The flies gathered on the outside of the glass and she wondered how to get rid of them.

Florida was sweating, lightheaded from the oppressive heat as she tried to remember what she knew about flies. She'd had maggot infestations before. They were born in refuse, lived on refuse and eventually, after a few weeks, turned into flies that she took great pleasure in swatting. But these maggots hadn't died like they were supposed to do and somehow they'd gone from the middle, little-white-wormy stage to huge annoying flies overnight.

Thinking in the heat became too difficult so Florida got up on shaky legs and stumbled to bathroom. She removed three litter pans from the bottom of the bathtub then closed the stopper and filled it with cold water. Finally, she settled down in the bath, felt cool relief and drifted off to sleep.

Hungry meows woke her and, looking out the bathroom window, she saw the setting sun through the veil of flies. "OK babies, I'll feed you. Shhh. I know it's late but mommy loves you," Florida cooed. Naked and dripping wet, she fed her cats, then with shriveled wrinkly fingers, refilled the tub and spent the night in the bathroom.

The next morning the flies were gone. Florida tentatively cracked open the door and found a cool, morning breeze that would keep the heat at bay for a few hours. She relaxed and swung the door open, stepped outside and gasped. "Jo?"

The cat lying on the driveway said, "Merow?"

Florida stepped toward the calico cat and shook her head in amazement. This cat was the spitting image of Jo, same markings, same meow, but she could tell immediately that this was a different cat. This cat was fat, not sickly. She approached this new kitty and saw flies hovering around and landing on its back leg.

The other cats wandered out of the house, rubbed against her legs and purred loudly like toy motorboats. Then they seemed to notice the new cat and the purring ceased. Florida watched them back away, backs arched, legs stiff. Then as one unit they ran around the corner to the other side of the house.

Florida shrugged, looked at her new kitty and said, "Cats. Whatcha gonna do?"

The new cat meowed in answer and Florida laughed. She grabbed one of the newspapers on the ground and waved the flies away. "Shoo," she yelled and the insects took off. She bent down to pick up the cat and saw it was injured. Its back haunch was cut and suddenly she was fighting nausea and revulsion when she saw maggots feasting on the wound. "Oh, you poor baby!" she whispered so as not to scare the cat. "Here, let me clean it."

She ran inside, grabbed some mismatched gardening gloves and soaked a rag in alcohol. Back outside she gently brushed the vile larva off the wound then, hugging the injured feline to her, she covered the cut with the rag. To her surprise the cat settled into her arms and purred instead of yowling and scratching.

"What a good baby," she cooed. "What a good kitty." She looked at the pile of wiggling maggots on the ground and squished them under her shoe.

"There now, let's get you inside and you'll feel better." She cuddled her new baby. She went to her bedroom and put him gently on the unmade bed. Using the same rag, she cleaned the wound again. "You look so much like Jo I'm gonna call you Maggoty Jo. You and me we'll just keep on killing those maggots and then all the flies. We'll show 'em who's boss! Right, Kitty?"

She sat in the living room with her new cat all day. When the others finally wandered back in for dinner, they kept their distance. They stayed on the opposite side of the room from Maggoty Jo. Florida frowned, annoyed at her cats for not welcoming her new cat. "Well, that's just fine, all of you can sleep out here tonight. I'm taking Jo with me." She grabbed her new cat and marched off to the bedroom, placed Jo on Ralph's old pillow and went to sleep with her newest cat purring away.

In the small hours, she woke to the sound of purring changing in tone to buzzing. The room was filled with flies, huge flies, stinging flies. Florida screamed and slapped at the insects, then jumped from the bed and ran from the room, slamming the door behind her.

She looked around and saw all her cats staring at her with unblinking eyes, then remembered Maggoty Jo. She yelped and ran to the door, then stopped. Those flies were in there and they were relentless. Blood was running down her arms and legs and as she touched her cheek she realized they were even on her face.

"Oh kitties, what can I do?" she wailed. "I can't let them kill her!" She stood at the door and waited for her hands to stop shaking and then opened it a few inches, ready to slam it if needed. To her relief, a paw grabbed the edge of the door and pulled it open a bit more. Then the calico squeezed out. Florida waited but no flies followed.

She walked away from the slightly opened door, hugging her cat and sank onto the sofa. Suddenly, the flies were back. They swarmed around her, biting her head, her arms and her legs. She slapped them away but they kept coming back until the pain grew too much. Florida passed out to the faint smell of the insecticide.

She woke to a sea of pain. Everything burned and as she tried to move, the flies that had been covering her flew off, leaving blood spatters over the floor and walls. She didn't know what was happening. The pain was bordering on unbearable. She weakly brushed at a deep gouge on her arm and her fingers came away bloody. She screamed. There were tiny eggs on her fingertips. How... what...

why... the questions were trying to come together but the pain stopped her from thinking clearly.

An involuntary shudder ran through her. Eggs! The flies were using her for a nest. Just like some dead animal! There was a strong pungent odor, a chemical odor and shuddered. She struggled to think a little better despite the acid-like agony eating away at her and realized the eggs smelled of the toxic insecticide. The maggots hadn't died from the poison she'd used. She felt dread filling her chest, they'd became stronger, the stuff must have actually accelerated their growth and development.

She knew she had to find the strength to get up and wash off every bite before the eggs hatched. She had to get up. Slowly, she sat and watched Jo come toward her. She looked at the cat and saw it was coming at her with an unnatural gait, stiff legged, staggering. Itt reached her feet and suddenly shuddered. She saw movement under its skin. She forgot about herself for a moment, the searing pain dulled as the cat opened its mouth and vomited thousands of quivering maggots. The smell was overpowering as the air became foul with the toxic stench of the bottled death she'd dumped on them just two days ago. She gagged and whimpered as the cat folded up and collapsed into a flattened pile of fur and skin.

Then the chemically tainted maggots converged on her, settling into all the wounds, all the openings they could find. She screamed until they filled her mouth and wriggled down her throat toward her lungs and then she wished she could scream some more as she waited to see what would kill her first, the maggots or the poison they carried.

When The Devil Knocks
Olivia Arieti

Gilbert was rubbing his hands in the attempt to warm them up. The winter was gelid and his fucking Cinderella garret even more. The fingers were so stiff that he couldn't help commiserating himself; he cursed his innate talent that had nourished dreams of fame and glory, the wasted years at the musical academy and the total lack of luck. His poverty was such that he couldn't even propose to Sophie, his gorgeous sweetheart; her father, a distinguished and wealthy gentleman, would have never consented to her marriage with the starving artist. Also the banging of the old shutters that made concentration hard were a malediction. He had to finish a stupid score for the local theatre's seasonal vaudeville, the only contract the bohemian wreck had been able to sign.

"Better perform in hell than in that squalid venue," he cried. "At least the flames would keep me warm."

The vision of the dauntless conductor directing a spectral orchestra in the infernal pit tickled his fantasy. Surely, the damned would have been a better public than the one he was about to entertain.

He was still lost in his bizarre reverie when hollow knocks made him jump up. Satan was at his door. An unpleasant smell of char entered with him.

"As long as your music drives your audience to perdition, you shall be the world's most famous musician," he promised and, after casting a glance at the squalor of the place, added, "also the richest."

The deal was sealed. From then on, the wantonness of Gilbert's notes stirred the fiercest emotions and unleashed all sinful desires to the point that his listeners, in delirium, were seized by a deadly thirst for gore that couldn't go unsatisfied.

Atrocity and horror spread quickly, the most gruesome crimes were committed and the devil rejoiced for the many souls recruited.

Not sated yet, he ordered him to work relentlessly. One concert followed the other, success and wealth were at the utmost but the tremendous fatigue had exhausted the guy.

One night the scores began seeping blood and the satanic notes came to life; the shadows of the hellish flames were already advancing.

Immediately Gilbert covered his ears but it was too late; the homicidal urge had taken hold of him as well. He found himself pacing the room like a madman before running into the kitchen where he grabbed the sharpest knife.

When Sophie, now his wife, called him to bed, he dashed up to her with bloodshot eyes and a frothing mouth.

On seeing him in such a state, with the glint of the blade already upon her, she cried, terrified, "Darling, what happened to you?"

The craving for blood had driven him wild and his stab silenced her forever.

When he came back to his senses, the sight of his lifeless spouse devastated him. Desperate, he pulled out the knife and plunged it into his chest.

At once, the diabolical creature crashed into the room and sneered to the dying maestro, "You've done an excellent job, man, and to show you my gratitude, I will also make your first wish come true; you shall perform for me forever."

At his command gigantic flames instantly enwrapped him and redness prevailed.

Journey Into Darkness
Stuart Holland

The fever had begun the day before and my temperature had been high, but not that high and there had been no cough, but instinct had told me, I was not well. That was earlier.

Now, as I slept, I dreamed, or at least I thought it was a dream, but it was more vivid than anything I could remember before this night.

The wind on my face was unmistakable. It felt cold, almost as ice, contrasting starkly with the fever I had been struck with during the day just gone. With the wind came the sound, unbearably loud, rumbling like thunder as it approached me. And then there were the lights, those soul-piercing lights as the train rounded the corner and thundered towards the place where I was standing. As it did so, it slowed and I noticed the number above the driver's window – 666. The number struck me as curious. With the train stopped, the doors opened with a hiss. I entered the carriage, realized instantly I was alone, and took a seat. The doors hissed again and closed behind me and the train departed the station.

And that was when I realized I was not alone and also the carriage was poorly lit. I could see no one but I was very much aware of a presence.

"Consignment UK202138001," the voice rang out as soon as we had left the station and entered the tunnel. "Are you consignment UK202138001?" The voice was urgent, even though if I had no idea what was happening.

"I have no idea. My name is Patrick Maudley," I spoke slowly and fearfully.

"Good enough. Consignment UK202138001…"

"What on earth do you mean. Why do you say I am a consignment?"

"All passengers on this train are consignments. Wait while I check the list… Yes your name and consignment number match. He's in here," the invisible voice boomed, as the door at the end of the carriage opened and a shaft of light penetrated the gloom of the carriage. The first thing I noticed was the light formed the shape of a tunnel. The second thing was how it slowly advanced towards me, in a paranormal sort of way. The third thing I felt was heat and then there was a burning sensation right in the middle of my chest as the light engulfed me. Finally I felt myself being swallowed and compressed so my chest felt tight.

I reached my hand up to grab my chest but it was no longer there. The carriage in which I sat had disappeared and suddenly everywhere was dark. Pitch black dark was all that was left.

I panicked.

I tried to sit up, but couldn't.

I tried to reach the glass of water I knew was on my bedside table, but I couldn't reach it. I tried to sit up again, but I was unable to move. Totally panicking now I tried to open my eyes in order that I might break the darkness, but my lids were firmly closed. And then I felt cold… as the voice from the carriage declared, "Consignment UK202138001 delivered. You have reached your destination. Gate 666 is on the left."

To Die For
Chris Rodriguez

"Why do bad things happen to me? I'm not a bad person," Rory mumbled as he bumped over the punishing back road. "It wasn't my fault! I'll kill Garafalo if I see him again. He never told me the bagman was a plant."

Rory had been traveling for a good ten miles or more down this wretched track without cell or GPS service. A twisted metal sign at the turn-off was barely readable since it had been used for target practice more than once. Who in hell would *live* in a god-forsaken place like this? Didn't feel like any hearth he had ever seen. More like Satan's icebox. *A couple days up and back, my ice-blue ass!*

He finally came to a turn off marked by a wooden rural mailbox. It seemed like another eternity before a massive iron gate blocked his entrance to an open courtyard fronting an ancient stone mansion. It reminded Rory of the haunted house movies he took his dates to see as a teen. There was even a thick fog hiding most of the residence from view. *Jeez, Freddie-friggin-Kruger must live here.*

I won't ever make another mistake. He felt an icy finger run down his spine knowing Mr. Mancini, the head of the family, didn't just fire his guys, he eliminated them. More than anything, Rory wanted to be back in the hot Miami sun.

He got out, popped the trunk and grabbed the loot. Eleven uncut, unmarked diamonds of the highest quality, supposedly one for each of the client's daughters – *eleven?!* Rory had to admit, he was intrigued.

He rattled the gate with both hands. It didn't open, but a shadowy figure appeared. The man, in evening wear, opened the gate and stepped forward.

"You must be Mr. Mancini's courier." He held out a well-manicured hand in introduction. "Maxim Canticle. This is my home."

Rory held out a mud-crusted paw, grimacing in apology. "Sorry, I took a fall back there. Had a flat. I would have called ahead, but there hasn't been a signal on my cell for a long time now.

Mr. Canticle smiled thinly. "We don't have service for the new gadgets out here, although we do have a landline phone. However, I'm afraid yesterday's storm brought down the lines and took out the power." He took Rory by the elbow. "You must be freezing. Please, come into the house."

Later, in dry clothes, in front of a roaring fire. Rory felt better, especially with an expensive cigar lodged in one scrubbed hand, a large brandy warming the other. Mr. Canticle entered a few minutes later and poured himself a drink.

"Would you like to meet my family? They've been asking about you. Not many visitors out here."

Rory shuffled his feet while pulling at the borrowed robe. "I don't know, Mr. Canticle, I'm not dressed…"

"Nonsense. We don't stand on ceremony in this house." Canticle chuckled. "At least not yet. I assume you understand we are celebrating a special occasion."

"Yes. The reason for the... the special delivery." Rory glanced over his shoulder.

"You brought them in with you?"

Rory removed the bag and handed it to his host. "All there. I'm sure you'll find them satisfactory. Mr. Mancini deals only in the best."

"Yes. Manny and I have shared a lifelong friendship." Rory watched closely as Canticle carried the package to a credenza. He poured the contents onto a dark cloth, revealing the flash of the jewels as they caught the firelight. "Exquisite," he breathed. He left them sitting open and went to the door. "You may come in now."

Twelve women filed into the room. The one in the lead walked over to Rory with quiet grace. "Hello, I'm Catherine Canticle. These are our daughters." She presented them by name and age.

The girls, aged 13 to 21, giggled when they saw Rory and chattered to each other. Then they stood dutifully behind their father.

"Can we see them now, Father?" the eldest asked. Her eyes shone bright, flashing like the stones on the dark cloth.

Rory was taken with her beauty. Her soft brown eyes were almond shaped and framed in the longest lashes he had ever seen but it was her shapely breasts that interested Rory most.

"Of course, darlings. Come choose which one you want. Christine first."

She looks like a goddess! Her flowing blonde hair was like a mane around her shoulders. Rory found it difficult to take his eyes off her lush form. He glanced briefly at her equally beautiful sisters. *Any man would be proud to boast a stable of these fillies.*

The girls squealed, giggling over their choices, but did not bicker. Rory thought it odd since he had three sisters who would have been fighting tooth and nail over this treasure. These girls seemed to know which jewel was theirs, claiming it with assurance.

Canticle grinned broadly, obviously pleased. "Well done, my lovelies. Now let's say good evening to our guest and get some rest. It will soon be time to ready yourselves."

Rory's eyes never left the girls until the door closed behind them. He finally turned to see Canticle watching him intently.

"My daughters," he said with clear intent, "will be married at midnight this night."

"Midnight? All of them? Isn't that a bit unusual?" Rory's brow furrowed.

"Tradition is important to us, Rory. We have observed this sacred ceremony for several centuries."

"I see," Rory replied respectfully, though he didn't see at all. "May I ask a question, Mr. Canticle? Why is this place called Satan's Hearth? An odd name for a home, isn't it?"

Canticle chuckled. "I always thought so. My great, great grandfather built this house on a rare underground geothermal spring. It was perfect for natural heating and hot water. The perpetual fog around the grounds is an unfortunate by-product. The locals back then claimed the water was heated by Satan's bellows in the bowels of Hell."

"Wow, that's quite a story. I suppose the name was a joke?"

"I admit my ancestor did seem to enjoy antagonizing the town folk. He wasn't popular in his time."

They finished their cigars and brandy in companionable silence.

"Let me show you to your room," said Canticle. "Your clothes will be cleaned and brought to you in the morning." Rory followed him up a long staircase to the second floor. "I'm afraid it will be a long night for us."

They entered a room with another lit fireplace. The bed looked comfortable. Rory's eyelids drooped. He had been a night owl from the age of 12 but his blood warmed by brandy and tired from the day's activity, he suddenly felt like he could sleep for a week.

"I'm afraid we must ask you for one more favor. I apologize for our caution. You understand. We have daughters about to be married. We can't take a chance."

Rory wondered what the old guy was babbling about. The light in the room was dim and Canticle's form seemed to melt. His vision blurred as he was lowered onto the mattress. *What was he doing*? Rory blinked hard, fighting sleep.

Catherine entered, carrying what looked like a large black sleeping bag. Canticle went over to assist. "Do you need to use the facilities before we tuck you in, son?"

Rory's mind couldn't quite grasp what he meant. He shook his head, too exhausted even to talk anymore. It took some wrestling as the couple tugged hard, pulling the heavy fabric over Rory's feet then all the way up to his neck. Catherine tied it at his throat.

"Do you know what we're doing?" Canticle asked as Catherine took out a large needle threaded with twine and began to stitch the bag closed around Rory's prone body. Almost paralyzed from his extreme fatigue, he simply rolled his head from side to side in denial.

Canticle smiled. "It's called bundling. Been used for centuries to protect the honor of women. Even though you are locked in a separate room, we can't take the chance. Our daughters *will* go to their husband intact. You do understand, don't you?" He ruffled Rory's hair before pulling the attached hood over the young man's head, leaving only his face visible.

Rory fought to keep his eyes open. It was very warm inside the bag. In fact, it was hot as Hell. He was trying to be polite, determined not to just pass out here and now. *He said, "...to their husband." Singular. Must be a slip of the tongue.* Not able to stay awake any longer, he slid into blessed oblivion just as he heard the lock click on the door. *For the girls' protection. The beautiful virgins, of course.*

Rory woke with a start. Heavy drapes obscured what little light the thin moon would have projected.

The fire was out. He licked dry lips but found no saliva to give relief. He blinked, trying to get his gritty eyes to adjust. He heard chanting from far away, not unpleasant to his throbbing head.

The bastard drugged me! The realization brought a new concern to Rory's fuzzy mind. *Drugged, locked in* and *bundled? Why the extra effort?* Rory knew the actions couldn't be merely to keep him away from the girls. *Why, then?* The whole thing was ludicrous. It was time to get out of here and go home. Rory struggled against the bag. He only succeeded in getting it uncomfortably twisted around his neck.

He lay still, listening. Unfamiliar music emanated from deep within the house. He didn't have to wait long. The doorknob jiggled, the lock clicked and when the door opened, Rory began a tirade.

"What the *blazes* do you mean by doing this to me?"

A large unfamiliar man stood in the doorway, dressed in a long black robe with a hood hiding his face. He didn't look friendly. A chill ran through Rory's now overheated body.

"I don't like this. Get this thing off me, *now*!" he ordered the stranger, assuming the man was a servant.

He didn't speak, just walked toward the bed, bent and picked Rory up like he was a rag doll. Rory pumped iron. He wasn't what anyone would call a lightweight.

"Come on, Frankenstein, put me down. Let me out of this get-up."

The man remained silent. He carried Rory downstairs to the front room. Soft candle and firelight glowed in the empty rooms. *What kind of wedding is this? No party?* This was the weirdest family he had ever seen.

"Hey, where are you taking me?" Nothing.

At the end of another hall, the man pulled a candle sconce toward him. A hidden doorway opened, stone steps led down into a cellar.

"Oh no you don't! I'm not going down there!" He bucked hard. The man held him easily as he took one careful step after another. Rory stopped struggling when he saw flickering light from around a corner at the bottom. He heard people talking in low voices.

The wedding! Why in hell would they have a wedding down in this dungeon?

They entered the massive room and, Rory noticed how high the ceiling was. Condensation dripped down the walls. *This must be the underground chamber with the geothermal spring.* He marveled at how many people it held. A couple of hundred at least. The strange thing was, they were all dressed in long black robes like the guy carrying him. Not too festive.

Jeez. These people are creepy, like vampires or something.

The crowd parted to let the big man carry Rory toward Canticle and Catherine who were standing on a stone dais above the guests. Rory was gently laid down on a rock. *It looks like a damned sarcophagus!*

Rory was creeped out. "What the hell's going on here, Canticle? Why are you doing this?"

Canticle placed a hand on Rory's head. "Calm yourself. You have been chosen to play an important part in our ceremony. You should be honored."

"Honored by what exactly? What part can I play if I can't move?" Frustration colored his loud voice. *Oh, my God!* he suddenly thought, *I'm not supposed to be the groom, am I?*

"Quiet, son. We have been celebrating this rare moment for centuries. The heavens are aligned in a perfect anomalous formation. It happens only once every 100 years. I saved my daughters for just this moment."

"This is ridiculous. Let me out. Now," Rory ordered as he kicked at the bag.

"It's too late." Canticle picked up a candle. "The portal has opened. We need to begin immediately."

A thundering roar sounded as the rock underneath him shook like an earthquake. A twisting spiral-shaped storm cloud appeared in front of the dais. Rory squeezed his eyes shut to shut out the rumbling. Then it stopped. A low murmur rose up from the crowd. Rory was surprised to see every person drop to their knees. Yellow smoke from the thermal spring swirled around the platform, obstructing his view, burning his eyes and nostrils. *Sulfur!*

Then a figure emerged, standing an impossible eight feet high. Muscled limbs rippled and pumped as the creature moved toward the rock – and Rory.

Rory's mind snapped. He shook his head, trying to make sense of what he'd seen. The thing standing before him was an image from books and pictures. He'd always thought it was the figment of frightened men's imaginations.

Canticle and Catherine bowed, moving toward the giant made even taller by the curled horns growing from a broad skull. Golden eyes narrowed as the couple handed over the velvet bag. The creature opened it and turned it upside down. Empty! The beast grinned, long yellow teeth gnashing as it grunted in satisfaction.

"Master, I give you my daughters, eleven jewels, for your pleasure."

The girls entered, dressed in simple white gowns. They came forward with bowed heads, each presenting a diamond to the monster. He opened his massive hand to receive the gifts, nodding with pleasure as he looked into the eyes of each girl. They knelt before him, fearless.

The creature then turned to face the Canticles. "What else have you for me?" it said with a voice Rory felt deep in the pit of his stomach, like the rumbling of the stone.

They turned toward Rory, extending their hands in his direction. "We give this man in your honor, Master. We hope you will accept him as our wedding gift to you from our good friend Mr. Mancini. This man's soul is yours."

Rory yelled out in fear. "No! No! What the hell do you mean? What are you doing to me?"

The beast grinned. "Mr. Mancini will be well compensated, as usual." It stepped aside as the big man picked Rory up again, then carried him down the steps and into the crowd. Rory screamed, bucking in desperation. A waste of effort.

The gathering drew back as a massive stone in the cavern floor rolled open with a scraping sound that grated on Rory's ears. Steam rose from a pool of bubbling water. He knew then what would happen.

He cried out, "Please, please! I didn't do nothing to deserve this!"

The last thing he heard was a splash as boiling water enveloped him. He felt his eyeballs harden to marbles, his throat melted shut forever. Seconds later, he felt nothing. His mind continued to scream the words his tongue was no longer able to release. "I didn't mean to make a mistake. It wasn't my fault!"

Gilded Demons
Terrie Avery

Time tracks into time on an unending loop that tips and rolls between the moments where decay laces in thick curds.

Here, I hide in folds of gloom-light and weep for you as your silhouetted shape trembles against wispy fingers of vapour curling over you.

Do you even remember when those gilded demons came?

I told you not to listen to their siren song.

I warned you not to follow those charming ones who roam the mountains of ruin and despair. I begged you not to let their veiled visions lure and beguile you.

Foolish, foolish, one, I cannot help you now.

I stay silent in the shadows, but they do not.

Harsh baying announces their arrival as they bound over jagged boulders, tearing at sharp granite and flaming brimstone as they come. It burns their gilded glamour away, revealing how deadly their leprous nature is. Not even the black-chained gates can halt their charge and the smoking metal and fiery-heated locks rattle and heave where they gather against them.

The sweet smell of you, helpless beside the gate, entices and excites them. You are the scented one, the pale soft flesh of their temptation, a trophy strung aloft upon the barbed tines of a thorn tree.

Crimson spittle flecks flanks and forked tongues flick over white teeth glinting in shadows, as they taste the murky air. The clamour rises, sending frenzied voices howling out into the void and setting deep echoes booming into the rolling dark.

One by one, they leap the gate and, stalking the scent of you, they circle the tree.

Death seeps into you but will not take you swiftly, for these creatures savour the fear and the game. Claws click, fangs flash and, still, time coils into those eternal moments on the unending spiral.

A hint of blood carries on shadowy-fired mist.

Dark warmth splashes cindered stone and I listen to your agony as they pick and peel. Your voice falters before the chords rip apart and skin trails away, from shoulder to belly and hip to ankle, in gauzy decoration. The sweet tang of blood intensifies, but I cannot help you.

Claws click again, opening flesh, pulling at the softness within.

Pulpy-eyed, almost sightless, your face dons its death mask.

I cannot help you now.

As I leave, an unspoken prayer dangles from slack lips.

The Gypsy's Curse
Mark Towse

"Who is it, Peter?" I hear my wife shouting from the back of the house.

"You pay," says the gypsy lady.

"No, I'm good, thanks. You have a great afternoon, though." I just wanted to get back to my whisky. It's already been a shitty afternoon—Jonathan on the phone. spitting out hate and lies to his mother.

"You pay!" she commands, with bite this time, shaking the basket in front of me.

What is she selling anyway? Wooden bloody clothes-pegs with drawn-on faces, bits of scraggy hair and dressed in cheap felt. Utter crap. No thanks.

"Look, I'm sorry, dearie, but I'm just not interested."

Did I just say dearie?

She furrows her brow as if mirroring my disdain and her near-black eyes shift into a new gear of intensity. Her severe demeanour is further emphasised by the tightly wrapped pale blue scarf around her head that pulls her grey hair in far too severely. Olive skin beneath sports a series of lines that look as though they have been chiselled in and the face is only slightly softened by a sprinkle of sunspots that run across the nose and cheeks. Yes, it all suggests a life harder than most. But impatience far outweighs my pity and my thoughts are already turning elsewhere.

Jonathan. Such a prick. He doesn't even know why he hates me but could never bear to be around—left as soon as he could. And he spreads his poison to all. I'm sick of it. He's not even my blood, but I still gave him a home. What more did he want?

"You a betting man?" she spits with a slight lisp, showing off her five remaining teeth in the process.

Why didn't I let Bec get the bloody door?

"No. Now, if you don't mind—"

One chance!" she says. "Give me one chance, Mister, and I'll be on my way."

Internally I sigh, but part of me is edgy about getting on the wrong side of this woman. She looks deranged. It isn't that I believe in folklore or mumbo jumbo, but why tempt fate?

She gives me that frightful smile again. "If I tell you something truthful, you buy one peg—one dollar for one peg. If I get it wrong, I will leave you to your evening. Deal?"

The basket only holds six pegs, so worst-case scenario, I'll be down six dollars.

"If I give you twenty, will you leave now?"

Her eyebrows meet in the middle and her face creases. I'll take that as a no.

I look behind me down the hallway, perhaps for support, but I'm on my own here. The warm glow of the living room mocks me, as does the soft drone of the television in the background. My whisky will be over diluted at this rate.

"Quickly then," I say with obvious frustration.

"Your hand," she says.

"Eh?"

"Your hand," she repeats.

For Christ's sake, that wasn't part of the deal. It's hard to tell if her fingers are just dirty or sun-damaged, but either way, the thought of those bony fingers touching mine fills me with disgust. Reluctantly, I offer it and she snaps her spindly digits around it with tremendous speed.

"It's so soft, like a lady's," she sniggers. Just when I think it can't get any worse.

She closes her eyes, launching into a bizarre on the spot dance, hopping from one foot to the next—the long colourful patchwork dress swishing around her heels. Now, she's humming.

Crazy bitch.

I spot a neighbour, Paul, peering through the window from across the road. He shrinks as we make eye contact, no doubt to mute the television and knock the lights off in preparation for a visit. Lucky bastard.

"Ha, just playing with you!" she screams, eyes wide and erratic. She performs a clumsy little twirl and takes a bow, obviously over-joyed at her little stint of improvisation. "Ready?" she finally asks.

Fuck me.

"Okay, first one," she says, stroking her chin.

First?

"Your name is Peter."

She has my attention. "How did you—oh, yes—of course," I smile. Thanks, Bec. "Fair enough, you got me. Here's the—"

She taps me hard on the shoulder. "You pay at end, okay?"

Another internal sigh. Is it too late to slam the door in her face? What's the worst she could do? Turn me into a frog. No, hang on, that's a witch. Fuck me, what am I talking about?

"I think that's enough for today, dearie." *That word again.* "Please take the dollar; I have stuff to do," I nervously mutter, edging the door slowly forward.

"It's Ruby. My name is Ruby. And the whisky can wait," she says.

My breath, she can smell my breath. She's sharp; I'll give her that.

"Well, it's been fun, Ruby, but—"

"Not finished. You pay at end." She sighs loudly, as though I'm taking up her time. "Rebecca. Your wife's name is Rebecca."

I must admit this woman has gone to town on her research, especially for the sake of a few pegs. It is creeping me out a little, though. She's probably just checked the mail. No, I brought it in this morning. Perhaps, she came earlier when we were at work or a previous day.

"Two pegs, Peter. You pay at end."

Before I can say anything, she smiles and says, "Jonathan is the eldest son, but he's not yours. The middle son is Matthew and the younger one is Phillip. Jessica's your only daughter."

I realise my fingernails are digging into my thigh. I'm beyond agitated, light-headed with confused anger, standing on the doorstep of my own home, but not in control. How does she know all this? This woman looks as far from internet-savvy as you can get. Has she been watching the house, spying on us? But Jon moved out over four years ago now—couldn't stand the sight of me. And how does she know he isn't mine?

None of this adds up, and for what? Pegs?

"Three so far, Peter. Three pegs. You can afford it, though. Done well for yourself by the looks of it," she adds, scanning the street.

My heart is pounding with adrenaline, and—is it fear that I am feeling? "Okay, I think that's enough now. You need to leave," I say firmly.

"Your mum died when you were sixteen," she says, still smiling.

The book. Of course—she has the book. Christ, she must be one of the few that has a copy. How else would she know? But what is this gypsy doing with my book?

"Four pegs, Peter."

"Look, lady—Ruby—this is a great little scheme you've got going on. I'm impressed. But I'm tired and I'd like you to leave now, please."

Her grip on my hand tightens and the eyebrows furrow further as if desperately trying to join forces. The eyes—they appear to be getting darker and her breathing is becoming faster, more excited.

I try and pull my hand away, but her vice-like grip gets even stronger.

"You still see her face sometimes when you are fucking your wife."

The perfectly manicured lawn across the road that usually provides a sense of comfort and safety is pulling away into the distance. I turn around to make sure Bec isn't in earshot, only to find a long dark tunnel is replacing our hallway, warm light from the living room becoming a distant beacon.

"Didn't get that from your shitty book of egocentric musings, did I, Peter?"

Fuck.

I step out onto the doorstep, gently close the door behind me and front up to her.

"Listen to me, filthy wretch. I've been nice so far, but it's time you fucked off now!"

It's an attempt to be forceful that comes out croaky and uneven.

"Five pegs, Peter," she says, finally releasing my hand. She begins to sniff at the air then, nose wrinkling and head darting erratically.

I snap the wallet out of my pocket, snatch the five-dollar note and thrust it towards her, but instead of taking it, she grabs my hand again and pulls me off balance towards her. "Ah, yes, the smell of fear," she spits. "Did you smell it on her, Peter?"

I move my face within an inch of hers and wrap my hand around her scrawny throat. "Listen, you fucking hobo; I don't know what you're talking about, but I'm warning you, take the money and go!"

"There he is." That smile again. "Old darkness coming out to play."

I feel so heavy I can barely stand. Bile rises, exploding in my throat as my stomach churns relentlessly.

"Stay with me, Peter; this bit is good."

Behind her, the grass begins to fade and houses sink into the distance. We're no longer in the street.

Even after all this time I still recognise the place—the moss-ridden graffiti on the walls, the smell of stale urine and the empty bottles of beer and whisky scattered around us.

"When you read in the paper that she killed herself, you felt nothing but relief."

I can see her—the girl and there I am too. We left the pub together, staggering and laughing and then I fucked everything up. How many times have I relived this in my head? I want to tell the old me to stop, but I know what's done is done. I hate myself—spent most of my life running from this monster I see in front of me, building a life I thought would protect me.

"Please, no!" I plead.

"Six pegs, Peter."

I try to fight it, but the dank claustrophobia and accompanying odour induce an explosion of vomit that doubles me over and leaves me trembling.

Christ, make it stop!

Stomach still reeling, visions of that night begin to swim through my mind—things I've tried to bury, but now emerging from their shallow grave.

But I've paid for this! Guilt has already taken its fair share!

"Who are you?" I ask, managing to croak the words out before the tears come.

"Her mother."

We are back. The smell of freshly cut grass fills my nostrils but provides no relief, only a heavy tangibility to the whole thing.

"There were never any charges—"

"They didn't care. She was drunk, so she was up for it as far as they were concerned. Her description was vague, fractured and they didn't even take it seriously. Nobody cared, and as you know, Amy committed suicide a week later. The case died with her."

"I'm—"

"Six pegs. Now, you pay."

I search for words, but they all seem so redundant.

"I've been waiting a long time to meet the man that raped my daughter. You ruined our lives, took everything away. I couldn't function. Out on the streets I was, until the gypsies found me. Took me in, helped me to heal, as best they could anyway."

My head is spinning. Nobody's going to dig up a case decades-old based on mumblings from some crazy old gypsy lady. But how does she know all this stuff? And how did we both end up back in that tunnel?

"Taught me some ways they did. Oh, boy, the things I've seen. Most people think gypsies just tell the future, but we also see the past. It took time to master, years, but then I saw, clear as day."

Words start spitting out of my mouth so fast, "I was young, stupid, inebriated. I didn't even know what I was doing. I am sorry that it happened, truly I am, but I think I've paid for it now. I tortured myself over it for so long, believe me."

"Not enough to turn yourself in, though, Peter. Make right from wrong."

"I thought about it—all the time. I did. I was just—scared."

"Took me a while to find you, too—new city, new state. A criminal lawyer now, huh? Sounds about right, a perfect match."

"I'm so sorry," I say, wincing at the inadequacy of the word.

"Six pegs, Peter. You pay now."

Nervously, I begin to fumble for my wallet, but she quickly grabs at my arm and places the basket of pegs in my hand. "Won't take your money, Peter," she says.

"Then what do you want?"

"For the debt to be paid." Using one of my shoulders for ballast, she draws in close and whispers in my ear, "Last chance to do the right thing, Peter. Leave the basket on the doorstep tonight. Life for a life."

And, just like that, she smiles, turns, and makes her way back down the garden path.

"What do you mean by that?" I shout.

Heart thumping wildly, still trembling, all I can do is watch as she walks down the street, patchwork dress clinging to her legs in the cool evening breeze. Finally, she turns the corner and is gone. I pause for a while, half expecting her to come back.

The house feels so warm as I close the door behind me and the sound of the television is a welcome relief from the old woman's throaty utterances.

"Bec!"

No answer.

"Bec, where are you?"

I place the basket on the hallway table an d notice the scribbles across the bottom of the pegs.

Curious, I examine them one by one. Each is marked with one of our names: Peter, Rebecca, Jonathan, Jessica, Phillip, and Matthew. Only one has been marked with an x on its side, though—Rebecca's.

"Bec!"

Still no answer.

I sprint into the living room.

It doesn't sink in at first—my mind still churning a thousand thoughts per minute. It's just too much to process—can't be happening—can't be real. Slowly, I draw close to her, reaching out towards the wooden hand. Features have been replaced with ink markings and a wide smile has been clumsily drawn across her wooden face. Her hair is made up of a few strands of brown wool, held in place by overly generous mounds of white glue. My wife is a wooden statue, inanimately seated in front of the television that still spits out images as though nothing is wrong with the world.

The living room begins to swim in and out of focus and voices from the television merge into a single deep drawl. I reach out towards the back of the chair to steady myself, but I'm not going to make it. The floor comes rushing towards me, the faces of my family flashing in front of me.

***

"Pete!" the voice sounds distant.

"Pete!" the voice again, closer now. I open my eyes and see my wife standing above me. The sight of her flesh and hair and animated features fills me with overwhelming relief. "Bec!"

"You passed out, scared me to death. What happened?"

"I—I don't know—perhaps the whisky."

"Who was at the door—before—who was it?"

"P—Pegs."

She frowns as she helps me back to my feet. It's so good to see her and I can't help but bring her in towards me. We stay like that for a while.

"Pete, what's wrong?"

"I'm okay, just glad to have you."

"You soppy old bugger."

Finally I let her go with a peck on the cheek, tentatively making my way towards the hallway.

Perhaps it was all in my head, a whisky induced visit from my old friend guilt, temporarily out of dormancy and delivering another of its suckerpunches?

Please, please, please!

I walk slowly across the carpet, eyes squinted, as though that might protect me from what's in store. And I pray.

The corner of the table comes into view and my heart starts racing, skin randomly beginning to sing with anxiety—and—oh fuck, there it is—the basket. I pick up the pace, rushing past the table towards the door, giving it as wide a berth as possible.

"Pete, what's going on?"

I turn the handle slowly and begin to pull the door towards me, craning my neck to peer through the gap. As soon I see what's left of the foul green liquid on the path, my heart sinks and I know none of this was in my head. Slowly, I edge back towards the table and the perfectly cut grass disappears behind the white of the doorframe.

Even before I pick up the pegs, I know what I will find and holding them towards the fading light confirms my suspicions, each one with a name written on its base.

"Fine. Just a bit dizzy. I think I need a lie-down."

"I'll bring up a nice cup of tea, love. You look so grey."

'Honestly, dear,"—*dearie*—"I'm fine."

I look into my wife's eyes and am overwhelmed with sadness. I have no idea why this woman loves me, but I'm grateful. I bring her in close again, once more holding the embrace for longer than usual.

Finally, I let her go, sombrely beginning to climb the stairs towards the bedroom. So, this is what it's come down to, after all this time, all this guilt. I've made many mistakes in life, but hasn't everyone? I know I should have turned myself in, but I think I've more than paid the price.

I grab a pen from the bedside drawer and pick up the peg marked Peter.

Her voice in my head, "Last chance to do the right thing, Peter."

***

Time flies. It's been nearly two weeks.

Every morning I check to see if the gypsy has collected the basket of pegs, but it still sits there. I daren't throw it or move it; I guess I'm more superstitious these days.

"Cup of tea, dear?" I chirp, making my way back to the living room.

My wife is smiling. I am growing to like that smile—the consistency—it was never like that before. And she's a much better listener, too. It felt good to finally get everything off my chest without fear of reprisal.

There were tears at first, but time heals and the guilt gets slightly easier to cope with each day. Hell, I've had my fair share of practice over the years.

The gypsy-lady knew I wouldn't be able to seal my own fate. She even showed me a glimpse of the future. I suppose she had hoped that I might still have it in me to change, but Jonathan is right; I'm weak, always taking the easier option. It even crossed my mind briefly to mark his peg, get rid of the poison, but the gypsy knew I wouldn't give myself the burden of a grieving mother. It would be relentless, unbearable.

I did love her, though, as much as I'm capable.

I told everyone that she left me, took some of her dresses and disappeared to Christ knows where. I don't think people know what to think. Jessica wants to believe mc, but I see some doubt in her eyes and I have Jonathan to blame for that. There's no evidence of foul play in my defence, though, and the police are just chasing their tails.

I'm getting good at this acting lark, too. My wife left and my brain broke and so on and so on. The wooden memorial in the living room helps my case for emotional distress.

We're having a romantic anniversary meal tonight. I have a special dress picked out for her, one of the few that I didn't burn. I take good care of her, even going over her with furniture polish yesterday. She came up really well, and I think she appreciates it.

"Just a minute, dear."

The doorbell used to startle me, make the hairs bristle on the back of my neck. It was usually the police or one of the kids for the first few days, but recently it's just been some nosy parker bringing a dish of food around or asking if they can do something to help. I guess they all want to check out the shoddy replica of my wife so they can tell their friends and have a good laugh.

Nobody's there. Perhaps it's kids messing with the street's 'crazy' person.

Only as I begin to close the door do I notice the basket is gone, replaced with a small fabric package wrapped in a pink bow. Surveying the empty street once more, I squat down, biting my lip to stem the sharp pain that runs down my right-hand side.

Even before I open it, I know it's a peg, but as I untie the bow and the material comes away, the sight of it and the x on its side still makes me reach for the door frame. I swallowed huge mouthfuls of air but not enough, I begin to rotate the peg with aching, trembling fingers, wincing as the pain in my side spreads across my chest.

It's over.

I know that even before I see my name on the bottom and read the accompanying note written on the inside of the fabric.

I gave you a chance, Peter. An opportunity to do the right thing. Even with a glimpse of what WOOD happen, you opted to save yourself. If you'd have just marked your own peg, I would have granted you redemption—the chance of a fresh start as a pardoned man.

The girls said I was too kind to give you a chance, but I knew you_WOODn't have it in you.

With a gust of breeze, the material breaks down into smaller pieces, escaping into the air like moths from a closet.

I try to scream but can't open my mouth. I raise a hand to my lips, noting my fingers are now just wedges of wood. Can't... feel... anything.

I try and push myself up, but I'm frozen in a crouched position, helpless as my skin begins to smooth over, concentric rings forming across every limb.

"Help!" My wife's voice from behind, panicked and distant, but no longer just in my head.

I can see, hear, but not feel. I'm present, but not; caged inside my new wooden prison.

What I *woodn't* give for one last chance.

Telling the Bees
Dona Fox

Uncommon light on my face woke me, then a soft rain refreshed my skin which had been dry for so long. Careful and slow I stretched first one leg then the other, bent my ankles, squeezed my toes. So stiff. How long had I been asleep?

The ancient house was collapsing around me– Odessa's Lodgings, named for my great-grandmother, my Gran. The old gray Queen Anne fanned out in two wings; one side was safe for me, the other had not always been.

Honeysuckle vines grew up beside the windows on the once dangerous wing of the house. It had been imperative that I stay away from the vines. I'd learned early on they were full of bees and I was quite allergic.

I had fallen into the vines once and it felt as if the bees had stung me in a thousand places. Mamma rushed me to the hospital where I almost died but for a hypodermic filled with a lifesaving dose of epinephrine.

The doctor said I was now either immune to the venom or that a single sting would kill me. He suggested we not play with fate by testing to see which it was and that we should tear the vines down and burn them that day.

But Mamma loved the scent so the vines remained and I talked to the bees from inside the glass. And the vines covered a larger part of the house every year, inviting yet a grander swarm of bees.

One reason I wanted to keep Mamma with me was that in choosing the vines over me she'd signed my death warrant. I wanted to compel her to watch my agony at the end.

I'd maintained her body with such care but they'd found her.

And with no one else around, of course, they'd blamed it on the boy.

I often wondered if he would give me away if he found the authorities more frightening than me. I'd done my best to terrorize him.

"I killed my Mamma." There, I'd told him. And from that day my son held one of my two greatest secrets–the darkest one, swarming in his chest.

"She shrieked and I clamped my hand over her mouth until she was too weak to scream. It happened so long ago, I remember nothing else from the night except my mother in her white gown, bubbles of red froth forming around the blade as her moans grew softer."

That's what I told him. Yet many more images remain vivid in my mind. How I climbed onto the bed and knelt in the flower that bloomed beneath her. And how, sobbing, I shook her. But she fell, limp and empty into the pool of blood.

"Her body pinned me to the crimson sheets as she murmured into my ear," I teased him with the horrific image.

"What did she say?" Big-eyed, my fearful son quizzed me. I could feel his heartbeat race as he backed away, afraid of me, his own mother.

I shrugged, "I don't know," though of course I did.

Clutching at my gown as her soul slipped from her eyes, my Mamma had whispered to me, 'what will you say when they come for you?'

"But what else could I have done, Lester? She was going to leave us the next morning. Without Mamma, who would take care of us? Who would run Odessa's Lodgings? I couldn't let her go."

My son looked at me with terrified eyes as I described how Mamma's blood covered the sheets and dripped onto his tiny lashes as he'd slept in his cradle beside the bed.

I splashed the rain against my cheeks then stretched my fingers. My, how my nails had grown! How long had I been sleeping? Dreaming…

Despite the rain-bright shaft of sunlight I bathed in, the corners of the room were dark, for my lodgings were within the walls. What woke me? Had some idiot come into our house again? We must be quiet, my loves.

At first, I thought it was another tour, soon gone.

I wanted to confront them and declare, "there's nothing supernatural going on here; not a ghost, nor a witch as some would say; but an actual person, just trying to get by on the stored foods in the cells until the boy comes home. If only you would leave me alone."–but then the jig would be up, wouldn't it?

I'd figured out how old I am, how much food we store in the basement, how many years I have left to live, how much I can eat each year before I die a natural death–in case the boy never returns. By my calculations, there's not enough canned food in the cellar but perhaps I'll die of a disease before starvation catches me. I fret.

Early on I made the mistake of trying to scare the visitors off, which only made it worse, made them more interested, more intent on studying the 'haunted' house.

Now I'm thinking maybe we should kill them all and they'd stop coming. I suppose there'd be ramifications, so no. We mustn't do that. Plus, they leave half eaten bags of chips and such.

But since they don't believe I'm alive, they wouldn't come looking for me, would they? No. They'd go interview my poor son again as if he can reach out from the hospital and murder willy-nilly.

Just so they don't alarm him. Please don't frighten the boy; he's a very timid child. He might spill the beans on me.

But then he'd already tried to implicate me, hadn't he? The Journal still hit the porch for a while after he'd gone and I read that they never believed Lester's ravings. He said I was the actual murderer but no one had ever seen me and they had found the letters from me, written from all over South America, promising to send for him someday. They'd overlooked the fact there were no envelopes, which would have had postmarks.

I peered out the window at the cause of my foreshortened nap. A thin young man stepped from a cab. He looked like a scarecrow. His haircut was ragged; he was tall and a cheap black suit hung loose from his bony frame. The poor thing was my son, Lester.

Had they let him out of the facility? Did they consider him cured? Was he coming home for good or was his return a trap? Should I reveal myself to him? No, he might be mad at me. After all, he'd had a lot of time to think and wonder why I hadn't stepped forward to save him.

Besides Mamma, there was also the matter of the girl Lester had sex with in the Crane Guest Room. I killed her with Mamma's kitchen knife–stab stab stab–as they described it. I wasn't in a frenzy. I'd calculated each step. I did it in the bathtub that time on purpose–so much easier to clean up afterwards.

I thought it wouldn't have been tasteful to wash the girl everywhere, not with the bleach, so there was irrefutable evidence pointing to Lester. So, they found him guilty of both murders and sent him to a facility for the criminal insane.

And now, here he was. He might be in a mood; I decided it was best for us to watch and wait.

"Mother!" Lester hollered as he climbed the sagging steps. He pushed the heavy door open and called again. His voice echoed in the front hall, "Mother! I know you're here."

If only I were a ghost, I could hide from him forever. No, there were no such things as ghosts. If there were, Mamma and that girl I murdered would be here hounding me day and night.

I smiled at my clever deduction.

No, I was real.

We had practiced being quiet as we lived in the tiniest of fissures between the walls.

The poor gangly man standing in the foyer calling for me was my son Lester. I should run to take him into my arms but I wasn't an idiot. Whereas before he'd feared me, now, I saw only bitter anger. As he waited his face grew darker until his cheeks were redder than blood running down the sides of a snow-white tub, so we continued to hide.

"Mother, I don't mean you any harm." Lester's voice was nervous-raspy and I could tell he was having trouble holding his calm exterior together. Then he ran for the stairway that led to the basement and his apartment.

I'd kept Lester's room dusted but changed nothing. He laid down on the bed, hugged his pillow to his face and sobbed.

At last, my big child raised his face and cried out to the room, "Mother, where are you? You let them take me away. You knew I wasn't guilty." He buried his face in the pillow again and tried to cry some more but he was dry. "Where are you, Mother?" He tossed the pillow across the room.

I put my hand on his back and he jumped.

"I'm sorry, Lester. They would have executed me."

"What?" He sat up, scurried away from me and pressed his back against the wall. He still feared me, or perhaps it was the knife in my hand.

"You're not quite right, Darling; I knew that would save you–not being well in your head." I tried to make my voice soothing and reasonable–to make up for the blade.

"What if they had found me sane, Mother?" He'd slid to the far end of the bed, his legs hung over, feet on the floor. We were having a rational discussion.

"Oh, they wouldn't have." Did he hear the edge of mirth in my voice?

"What guarantee did you have of that?" He stood up as if he were growing a backbone after all.

"Oh, my poor foolish Lester." The look in his eyes told me running was a better alternative than trying to grab the blade off the floor. I felt my foot tangle with his then I watched the cement floor rise to meet my face.

When I came to, he'd bound both my hands and feet to a wooden chair which faced a window.

I could smell food cooking; there went my careful rationing. I had to get free before Lester killed me; for I knew he was insane and capable of murder.

It was my fault he was a terrified child. I'd made him that way. Now he was a fearful adult. I worried he would try to assuage his fears by unmasking me, the actual monster, to the law or worse, he'd try to kill me himself in a fear-crazed frenzy.

Then I smelled honeysuckle, so strong it overrode the smell of the food.

This was a room where the fragrant vine grew over the window panes—and the lower sash was open.

My struggle tipped over the chair Lester had bound me to and I landed with my cheek against the casing. There was a high-pitched whine as a solitary bee settled on the sill right beside my face. Another joined it, then another. I could hear the murmur in the wall and I watched as the bees walked on my skin and crawled beneath my clothes.

My hands were bound behind me and my feet were tied to the legs of the chair. I tensed all my muscles to force my body from the window, then I felt a dozen searing needles slide into my flesh and deliver shock-waves to my nerves–the jolt gave me the final impetus I needed to get free.

When Lester came into the room, I was shaking and covered with red welts as if a lover had been suckling at my flesh. He shut the door behind him and I recognized the drug that had once saved my life. Yes, sticking out of his shirt pocket was a hypodermic just like the one that had administered a lifesaving dose of epinephrine to me when I was a terrified little girl.

But now my reaction to the stings was so far progressed the hypodermic would have been unlikely to affect me. Perhaps Lester thought it could slow my body's response until he got me to the hospital–but he had only one hypodermic that I could see–so maybe the injection wasn't for me but for himself–in case he got stung.

I was having difficulty breathing, my heartbeat was rapid and I was dizzy–all the same feelings I remembered from intense bouts of sexual activity with Lester's father. Even so I noticed something wrong with the way Lester looked. Was that Lester, or was I hallucinating? Was that my Gran? I thought I was watching an old woman with a bandana tied under her chin. It didn't matter. I needed to get out of the bonds, and fast.

"Are you going to give me the shot?"

"No." Now I saw the figure was indeed Lester. He was bouncing on his toes and kept looking at the doorway.

"Then we should go to the hospital," I wheezed.

"No." He backed toward the door, then took a sudden step to the window.

I needed a drink, my tongue felt too large for my mouth but I needed to know. "What will you say when they come for you?"

"I can't understand a word you're saying." Lester slammed the window shut then pulled the curtains together in one brisk motion. He tore the bandanna off his head and swatted at the drapes with it.

The room spun as Lester twirled. Perhaps it had gone too far this time; I needed to vomit, but my throat was closed. Was I going to die this time?

"Do you like my clever get-up? I'm practicing being you, Mother." Lester wrapped the scarf over his head and tied it under his chin like an old woman and finished with a laugh.

I felt my body go rigid then watched as my arms and legs jerked against my bonds, quite outside my control. Ah, this was the best part–my climax–too brief. It would soon be over.

"We have guests, Mother. I'm eating with them tonight and checking them out in the morning, but I'll prop you up so you can see them off from your window."

Lester talked like a tape recorder on double-speed. He bent to kiss my damp forehead and didn't notice as I knocked the hypodermic out of his shirt pocket and onto my lap. Probably not in time if I needed to be saved, but just in time, it was a feat I couldn't have accomplished one second later if all was going as Lester thought. I rolled my eyes up, then trembled my lids shut and peeked out of tiny slits.

"Goodnight, Mother dear." He ran across the room and began fumbling with the door knob.

He couldn't get the door open and a trail of bees had followed him. He must have realized they were also in the scarf tied around his head. He started jumping and twirling more frantically than he had before–he couldn't get the scarf off and thrown away fast enough.

I had passed the severity of the allergy to my son.

Lester shrieked and clawed at his shirt pocket, but the hand that had slipped from my bonds now hid the hypodermic in my lap. He screamed as dozens of vibrating bees touched their tiny black stems into his soft flesh.

I am no longer threatened; I am loved.

The son I feared for so long, because of what he might say to find his own comfort, will keep my secrets forever. I am no longer afraid of his fear. They didn't believe him before and he won't be speaking again.

The ancient rope Lester used to bind me didn't hold long enough for us to be caught out.

The bees have not harmed me. Over time they became my lovers—we live in the walls together. Sure, they sting me but it's not abuse—it's good for me. The stings invigorate me, goad me on when I would become complacent.

It's like living with a lover who forces me to experiment with drugs that are quite strong. I hold on and ride out the affects to please that lover. Because we share better times.

I'm addicted to the icy chills of hunting and of murder. Each delicate hair on my body shivers when their tiny feet clutch my skin as they layer themselves like a robe on my pale flesh. Then we go out and hunt in the night as one.

We gorge on the meat together so I know they need me too.

Someday they will want to feed on my living body, I shall let them have a taste—the whole swarm—but there are thousands of them and more each day so each of them may have just one tiny bite from my flesh—that's what I shall say when they come for me, that's what I say, Mamma.

Stealing Souls
Justin Boote

Darren Barmsby checked once again no one was looking, then started excavating the grave. The deceased had only been buried that morning which made his job a lot easier, but this wasn't his primary reason for digging up this one. He'd watched the funeral from afar, hiding in his little makeshift hut with a pair of binoculars, scanning the mourners. All of them had been wearing expensive outfits, shiny jewellery which looked brand new and more importantly, once the service was over, they had all left in their also shiny Mercedes, BMW's and even a few sports cars. Darren was pretty sure one had been a Ferrari when it had started up then roared off. This told him one simple thing—the woman that had been buried had also been rich and it was all he needed to know.

It was dark now but being grounds-man of the same graveyard meant he knew his way around with his eyes shut. He'd been working here a long time and the nice little side-line he had, digging up the recently buried and taking with him whatever expensive possessions they'd been buried with, was also something he'd been doing for a long time. He'd gotten it down to quite the art by now; watching the crowd to assess their status, waiting until the graveyard was closed in case any bereaved relatives were reluctant to go and ensuring that when he'd finished, the soil and grass was left exactly as he'd laid it in the first place. Darren didn't like the idea of spending time in prison for grave-robbing. He shuddered at the thought of what the inmates would do to him if he did. What his mother and father would think. He told himself he would commit suicide rather than face the shame and embarrassment, but the fact was the buzz and adrenaline rush, plus the lucrative aspect, made it hard to resist.

Darren stopped when the small shovel connected with solid wood and went about the task of opening the coffin quickly and efficiently. This was the dangerous part; he could figure an excuse for digging up the grave but snooping around inside was a tough one to explain. He prised open the lid and there she sat—the elderly lady who had died of cancer. Around her neck was what he took to be an authentic pearl necklace and the diamond on her ring just had to be real, too. The huge diamond. He took both, shoved them in his pocket and within minutes the hole was covered up again.

His heart thudding as always, his body shaking with the exertion and nerves, he finished tidying up the area and was about to leave when movement at the back of the graveyard caught his eye. Someone was watching him.

He gasped, recoiled in shock and ducked down behind the gravestone. Who the hell was in the graveyard with him? Some young kid with his girlfriend? Wouldn't be the first time he'd caught horny couples in here. He dared to peek over the top of the gravestone again. There it was, the long dark shadow beside a tree, motionless, yet somehow he knew it was looking his way.

He thought of playing dumb, doing his job and chasing after the intruder, but what if it wasn't some harmless kid, or even a homeless person looking for somewhere quiet to sleep? This happened plenty of times, too. What if it was a relative of the deceased come to pay further respects and had stumbled on him digging up her grave? Maybe he was on the phone to the police right now.

That was enough for Darren. He picked up his tools and scrambled out of the graveyard. Once he'd jumped over the wire-mesh fence, he turned back to see if he was being followed. He wasn't. Whoever it was remained in exactly the same position and stance which made Darren wonder if it might be one of those huge, carved angels people sometimes had as gravestones. But he knew every inch of this place and over there, beside the tree, there were no angels. Only squirrels and owls occupied that particular area. He ran.

After an hour or so, when there were no knocks on the door from the police or irate family members, Darren finally relaxed. He pulled out the necklace and ring he'd hidden under the floorboard upstairs and took them downstairs to study. He wasn't an expert but there was no doubting these were real and had to be extremely expensive. There was a good two week holiday somewhere warm to come out of this. He congratulated himself on a job well done, finished his whiskey for both his nerves and celebratory means then headed up to bed.

Tomorrow he'd go straight to his friend who handled goods and start looking where he might spend his holiday. The Bahamas sounded good.

He lay in bed and tried to get to sleep but it was nearly impossible—his head was spinning with the idea of a proper holiday for once. He considered another couple of shots of whiskey to help when he heard a noise downstairs. A shuffling sound, heavy, as though someone was moving the sofa. He sat upright, heart pounding, ears straining for further sounds. Something fell to the floor and smashed—a vase or something.

"Shit!" He was being burgled. He looked around for his cell phone to call the police then realized he'd left it downstairs. He had no choice but to confront the intruder. Darren wasn't a big guy and was definitely not the fighting type so he searched for something big and heavy to hit the guy with.

The stairs creaked.

he grabbed a wooden chair and held it above his head, accidently scraping it along the wall just as the bedroom door flew open. He yelled at the intruder, rushed towards the door and out onto the landing, then stopped. There was nobody there.

Darren spun around, expecting the guy to be standing behind him, surely about to stab him or worse and was both shocked and surprised to see he was the only person There.

"What the hell?"

A thud came from the kitchen.

Darren ran downstairs, conscious that he'd clumsily left his precious jewellery in a drawer in the living room, which in turn gave him the confidence to confront whoever was in his house. He ran along the hallway, chair above his head, into the kitchen. Nothing. He ran to the living room. There on the floor was the broken vase and the sofa which had been moved slightly. The necklace and ring were thankfully still in the drawer but now he was perplexed as to how the intruder had gotten in and more importantly out again without breaking a window. The front and back door were locked and there was no smashed glass anywhere.

He started wondering if he had imagined it all instead but the remains of his vase were there and his bedroom door hadn't opened by itself. Or had it?

He'd worked at the graveyard for almost twenty years and not once had he ever considered anything remotely supernatural occurring. He didn't believe in ghosts; once dead, you stay dead was his belief, so the idea it had been anything other than a burglar he refused to consider. And yet...

"Bullshit," he mumbled. The guy had escaped because he had found an open window somewhere or quite simply, the door wasn't locked. So why was it locked now, then?

"Because I just locked it myself in my panic and didn't realize."

This was good enough for Darren, so he grabbed his jewellery, took it with him upstairs and went back to bed, but not before another two quick shots of whiskey. He was asleep within minutes.

When he opened his eyes the next morning he felt strangely fatigued as if he'd hardly slept all night.

This was weird as he didn't recall any bad dreams and thought he should be feeling quite refreshed. He had stuff to sell and a holiday to think about. As always after he'd stolen from the deceased the first thing he did was check his bedside table to ensure the jewellery was still there. He picked it up, got dressed and put it in his pocket before heading downstairs. And froze.

The entire living room was in disarray. The sofa was upside down; all the drawers in his cabinet were open and everything thrown onto the floor. The kitchen was the same as was the dining room. He quickly checked the doors and windows, all were locked.

"What the hell's going on here?" he asked the empty house. Instinctively, he fumbled the jewellery in his pocket, thanking God he'd thought to take it upstairs with him last night. Nothing was missing from his house—the T.V., DVD player, his laptop, everything was there. Then he thought back to the shadow which had been watching him the other night at the graveyard. There could be no doubt a family member of the old woman had followed him home, but for what reason he didn't know. Either he was angry about Darren digging her up or he wanted the jewellery himself.

"Well, you ain't getting it!"

As if in answer, the bedroom door slammed with such force he swore the whole house rocked. He was sure he heard distant screaming or howling. He bolted upstairs, threw open the door and burst into the room. Nothing there.

"What the fuck's happening? Where are you?"

He turned in circles looking for whoever was harassing and taunting him. A shadow moved abruptly out on the landing. He ran back out, saw nothing then dashed to every room upstairs, swinging the doors open but again, nothing.

By now panting and feeling both nervous and angry at the same time, he decided to get out of the house and sell the jewellery before he went completely mad. He reached the bottom of the stairs and stopped. There was a man in his kitchen.

Darren froze. He had started convincing himself that there might actually be a ghost after all causing all the trouble, but this was no ghost. The man was holding a large kitchen knife that sparkled as he waved it from side to side. He was wearing a hood, was completely dressed in black but his face was most definitely human—his eyes wide and bloodshot as though on drugs.

"Where is it?"

"What? Where's what? Who the fuck are you? What're you doing in my home?"

"You took it. I want it. It's mine, not yours. You give it back or I'll slice you a new mouth, you thieving piece of shit."

Anger replaced Darren's original shock. It had been an intruder after all, not stupid notions of ghosts that had him questioning his own sanity. The guy was bigger than Darren, much bigger; it didn't seem there was a lot he was going to able to do if a confrontation occurred.

"I don't know what you're talkin' about. Get outta my house before I call the police."

"Oh yeah? That's not a bad idea. We can tell them how you stole my grandmother's necklace, you fucking ghoul."

What to say to that? There wasn't any point in denying it and it was still too early in the day to say he'd already sold it. It looked like that holiday to the Bahamas was going to have to wait, after all. And yet...

"The necklace, you say?"

"Yeah, the necklace. I want it. What's the point of a dead woman wearing it? Hardly gonna use it, is she?"

The guy branded his knife again and stepped closer.

Darren thought of running, but what good would that do? Besides, it appeared it wouldn't be a complete disaster. Maybe... just maybe...

He pulled out the necklace and threw it at the intruder who deftly caught it and stuffed it in his pocket. The guy stared at Darren for a few seconds and he was sure his last vestige of hope was going to die, too. Instead, the guy turned and headed out the house.

Darren pulled out the ring and held it up. The burglar hadn't known about that! This alone had to be worth several thousand. Now considerably more cheerful than he'd been earlier, but still not quite believing his luck in what could have been a disaster, he waited until he was sure the guy had gone then headed off to sell it.

***

Darren was drunk by the time he decided to go to bed that night. He'd gotten more than he had expected for the ring and had booked himself a two week stay in the Bahamas, starting next week. His boss had been fine about such short notice, all he had to do was wait for the next three days to pass so he could get the hell out for a while.

The wad of notes sat heavy and comforting in his pocket and he was reluctant to remove them, but even though drunk, he was still conscious of how easy the intruder had gotten into his home. He stumbled around the house, locking the doors and windows then headed upstairs where he put the money inside his pillow. No one was going to find it there. He lay in bed, already half-asleep and thinking about Mojitos and scantily-clad girls when there was a thud downstairs.

Darren's eyes shot open.

His immediate thought was the burglar had remembered the ring and had come for him. His stomach dropped, thinking of the money under his pillow and of being forced to hand it over. There was no way; he'd fight if he had to. Another thud followed then something heavy being dragged across the floor. A glass or bottle smashed, sounding like an explosion in the silence of the night.

"Fuck this. No way. I'm not having this!" He jumped out of bed and headed to the landing. A noise, like someone breathing heavily or hissing, came from the living room. Darren rushed down the stairs, trying to keep as quiet as possible and grabbed the coat hanger by the front door. He threw off the coats and raised it above his head, ready to smash the intruder's head in.

Loud panting came next; the guy obviously exerting himself looking for the ring, not caring if he woke Darren. Well, he was in for a shock this time. Darren burst into the room and swung the coat hanger wildly around. It was several seconds before he realized there was no one there.

The living room was once again a mess. The sofa was overturned in the far corner, all the drawers from the desk by the mantelpiece had been emptied—their contents were everywhere. The half-empty bottle of whiskey was a thousand shards of glass, the potent contents wafting to greet him.

"Where the fuck are you?" he screamed. "Come on! You want it, come and get it!"

A shadow darted across the adjacent dining room.

Darren yelled and chased it. "Hey, you want the ring, take it off me!"

The shadow rose on the stairs. It was impossible to tell if it was the same guy or not, but it had to be. What Darren couldn't understand was why he didn't confront him. Why hadn't he run off now Darren had caught him in his home? Maybe he was trying to lure him somewhere so he could hit him, or stab him with that huge knife of his. Well, not gonna happen, he told himself.

As Darren headed up the stairs, a large knife in his hand, too, he called up to him again, now tired of chasing him. "Hey, you're wasting your time. I already sold the ring. And I've spent the money so get out!"

He stopped halfway up the stairs to listen. Would the guy now come out, confront him? Instead, an immense resounding crash shook the foundations of his house. Paintings fell from the walls and the ceiling light rocked violently back and forth. Darren grabbed the bannister, sure the stairs were going to collapse beneath him. A howl that pierced his heart and threatened to burst his eardrums caused him to recoil and almost fall again as he covered his ears.

The shadow, now huge and ominous, covered the whole upstairs landing, turning everywhere dark, blotting out the ceiling lights. A crash and thud, which sounded as if a meteor had just fallen through the roof, made the walls shake, bits of plaster falling onto Darren like giant snowflakes. He forced himself to confront whoever was doing this; if not they were going to destroy his home. Besides, the money was still under his pillow.

He dashed up the remaining steps, using the idea of having his money stolen to give him the courage to confront the intruder—they were doing a lot of damage up here. A stench—potent and terrible—oozed from his bedroom, as though something huge had died in there and had been left rotting for months. Darren gagged and pulled his t-shirt up over his face, the knife held high ready to swing.

Then, he took a deep breath instantly regretting it and burst into his room.

And immediately recoiled, tripped over his own feet and fell against the wall.

He tried to babble a question but the words failed to come in a coherent manner; instead a series of garbled sounds followed. This was no burglar standing there in his bedroom, the notes from inside his pillowcase scattered everywhere and blowing around the room. The woman, the one whose grave he had dug up and stolen jewellery from, swayed back and forth beside his overturned bed, one moment cloud-like and semi-transparent; the next as solid as he was.

Her white eyes, missing any other colour or pupils glared at him, exuding rage and menace. She looked at the bedside table and this immediately rose into the air and exploded, showering them both in its contents. A withered, gnarled and bony arm raised and pointed at him, trembling slightly. Already, despite having been buried only the day before, her skin was drooping as though she was melting. Her long grey hair, which had previously laid over her chest and bosom like a delicate shawl, now waved anarchically around her head and face.

"Where is my ring?"

Darren whimpered, unable to comprehend what he was seeing.

"You took my ring. I want my ring!"

He shook his head, still unable to physically tell her he was sorry, he had sold it, if he had known…

She glided over the bed towards him, staring down at him, tendrils of her smoky substance brushing his face and smelling of decomposition.

"Gone," he managed. "Sold. Sorry."

Another screeching howl echoed around the room. Darren cowered, covering his ears again, wishing he could go back in time and return everything. More spectres appeared; the old man with the gold watch; the young woman with the silver necklace; another old woman with the gold rings. They swarmed over him, brushing him with their wispy forms. Then, as one, they all howled together and dove into Darren's body. He could feel them swishing and swirling around in there as though his bones were snakes trying to bite their way out. The last thing he recognized before he fell unconscious was the intruder from before, standing there shocked and wide-eyed at his bedroom door, no doubt having returned for the ring, too.

***

When he opened his eyes again, the room he found himself in was stuffy and pitch black. He tried to turn over but he couldn't move. Had he been paralyzed as revenge by the ghosts of those he'd stolen from? A crunching sound ensued, then more, coming from above. The sound of multiple tiny things hitting hard rock or wood. And then, as he recovered his senses more and he felt around, he realized where he was.

He banged on the roof the coffin as more soil was thrown down. He tried to push the lid off with his knees, knowing already it was futile; coffins were not designed to be opened from the inside. His panic now total, he scraped at the lid, then looked in the pockets of the clothes he'd been buried in. Someone, he didn't know who, had dressed him in his best suit, one he hadn't worn for years. He pulled out a small object, his grandfather's silver Zipper light he'd given to him as a child.

He ignited it, hoping and praying he could burn a hole in the coffin, but once again, dismay and horror sunk in when it saw it was metal —as, again, he'd already subconsciously known it would be. Around him on the floor were the notes which had been in his pillow case. Thousands of Euros now as useless as ultimately everything had been to him. He had been buried with his most precious possessions, just like all the others. Then he saw the necklace beside him. The intruder had returned it. Had he, too, been tormented by its owner? Had come to return it so all the blame lay on Darren? Then, he'd assumed he was dead and had called the police, wanting to be rid of any connection to his dead grandmother.

His final thoughts as the air was sucked from his lungs was of the burglar. Would he be watching now from afar as he had done so many times? Would he rescue him in time or would Darren be a dead, cold corpse when he prised open his coffin? All because he had wanted to take a little holiday somewhere warm.

Had that been too much to ask?

Canvassing
Michael B Fletcher

I looked at my finger, its normal skin colour covered by a thick crust of paint; pinks gone to green and grey, life gone to decay.

I held it to the light, vertical, to watch the liquid begin its slow slide to the floor. But it stayed, hardening, refusing to move from its position, refusing to acknowledge what I'd done.

'Another day, another life on canvas,' I hummed as if it'd make the slightest difference. The light passing over my shoulder lit the deep recesses of the room, casting illumination over the rolled bundle in the corner. I squinted, ignoring my finger for the moment and then smiled.

No way anyone would know what that was, Just a bundle of canvas in an untidy studio room. Yes, safe enough until I can dump it.

A knock downstairs grabbed my attention, causing me to run my hands down my overalls and smear the caked paint along my leg. *No,* I thought calmly and moved towards the door. *Nothing untoward, just a painter painting. What you'd expect.* I took my time descending the stairs.

Another knock, more impatient.

'Coming!' I called, though I didn't hurry. They, whoever it was, could wait.

The frosted glass of the front door revealed two men, dark clad and official. I pondered who they might be and why they were at my door. I had few visitors, virtually never any buyers, just the occasional person usually trying to find someone I didn't know.

'Mr Theros?' The voice was deep and authoritarian.

I reached for the catch and slowly opened the door.

The uniform was somewhat of a shock but I showed no reaction, just stood there. 'Yes?'

The thinner of the two officers nodded and smiled at me. 'May we come in?'

I had no wish to have anyone in the house, particularly from law enforcement so remained blocking the doorway.

'Why?'

The second man sighed. 'We've reports of a missing person, a young woman who was last known to be in this neighbourhood and we're canvassing the area. Have you seen her?'

'No.' I began to close the door.

'I think we should chat some more,' said the first man. 'We have a few questions.'

'If you must.' I reluctantly stood back as they entered.

'How about a cup of coffee?' he asked.

'I haven't much time,' I answered, 'I'm in the middle of painting. The canvas will dry out if I leave it too long.'

'I'll put the kettle on, shall I?' the first man asked as he walked into the kitchen. 'We've time for that, surely.'

I took a deep breath and followed them into the room. 'Be quick then.'

The larger officer sat at the table and pulled out a notebook while his companion turned on the jug.

I took my favourite chair so they would look into the window's light and attempted to appear relaxed.

'So, Mr Theros,'.

I raised an eyebrow. 'What!'

The thinner man busied himself looking for cups in the wall cupboard.

'You're a painter?' the man looked up from his notebook.

I held up a paint-caked hand in reply.

'So, we're searching for a young woman in this area and believe you might be able to help us.' He passed over a photo. 'As you see, she is attractive.'

I held up the photo and couldn't help admiring the bone structure of that face, blond hair framed over dark eyes. *An artist's model in fact.*

'No, haven't seen her.' I flipped the item onto the table. 'Is that all?'

'Here's your coffee,' said the thin man, placing a chipped cup filled with dark liquid in front of me. 'Couldn't find any milk, but I don't mind black. Name's Oscar, by the way. My partner's John.'

He sat, cradled his cup and looked at me.

'So, what sort of painter – modern, landscape, impressionistic, portrait?'

'Uh,' I paused, giving myself time to think, 'I'm more of a traditionalist, I suppose.'

'Do you mean you draw people?' Oscar asked while his partner wrote something on his pad.

I looked up to the ceiling while seeking a neutral answer. 'I can, occasionally…'

'Well?' A voice attracted my attention.

I reluctantly dragged my focus to their intense faces. I needed to satisfy their inquiries and get them out. My eyes flickered up and I noticed a crack making its way across the age-stained surface. A dark drip hanging there caught my attention.

'Why do you want to know that? I do a range of things but most of my painting income is more of what you can see, recognise.'

'You mean, like people!' Oscar was persistent.

'Whatever is required or commissioned. Have you finished your drink? I've a lot to do. The paint will be too dry to allow me to complete my work if I'm away for too long.'

'Don't let us delay you. Why don't we take ourselves into your, ah, studio? We can talk while you work.'

I WAS sure he was provoking me, but I wasn't having it. They had to go, now.

'No, I need to work alone. Important for my creativity.' *Damn, the drip's bigger, about to drop.*

'Take another look at the photo.' Oscar pushed it across the table surface.

'I'm sure I haven't seen her. Can't you take "no" for an answer?' *The beautifully structured Nordic features were hard to forget, once seen.* I kept my face impassive as I shook my head.

'Uh, finish your coffee. Please.' I tried to keep the urgency out of my voice. I knew that while paint would dry quickly, other liquids would not and the ceiling crack was a concern.

I felt tightness across my shoulders, a situation out of my control.

Oscar got up, still holding his cup. 'I'm keen to see your work,' he smiled. 'What about you, John? Mr. Theros shouldn't mind.' He looked down at his companion.

Suddenly the drop fell from the ceiling, fortunately while they were looking away. But I saw it, hitting next to my cup. I watched the droplet spread, crimson.

'No, not at all!' I rushed to the door. 'Be happy to show you some of what I do. Come on then.'

'Fine,' added John, folding his notebook and standing.

I hurried through the door and put a foot on the stair. Fortunately they had followed, taken in by my quick movement. I ascended the stairs at speed as they began to climb.

'No hurry, Mr Theros, no hurry.'

I ignored the thin man's platitudes as I scanned the room. Just untidy enough to look appropriate and the roll of canvas not showing any visible staining. *Yes, all as it should be,* I thought as I waited.

Then I saw the portrait awaiting the final touches to her face.

Damn!

The policemen clattered into the room as I threw a light drop cloth over the painting. 'Not much to see,' I waved a hand around the room.

They stood, slowly scanning my studio. Nothing appeared to attract their attention.

"What are'ya painting?' John jerked his head towards the covered canvas on the easel.

I hesitated until I saw Oscar start to walk towards the darkened corner of the room where the pile of canvas waited. 'Fine!' I announced loudly, 'I'll show both of you. Anything so I can get on with my work.'

Fortunately Oscar turned back.

I partially pulled the drop cloth from the painting, revealing a portion of the reclining nude. 'I won't show any more if you don't mind as it's bad luck to reveal an unfinished painting.'

'Don't be modest,' said Oscar catching my hand and dragging it and the rest of the cloth away. 'Wow, not bad, eh, John. Yet to finish the face, though. But still she looks familiar, doesn't she?'

'One model is much like another,' I interjected attempting to recover the blonde's full figure.

'But she's very like the missing woman, eh, John? Very like.' Oscar added, taking a sip of his cooling coffee.

"I'm not that good a portrait painter,' I said quickly. 'There are similarities, I agree, but it's not her, I assure you.' I managed to cover the canvas without interference. 'But if I come across her I'll let you know.' I held out an arm to usher them out.

To my relief they preceded me down the stairs to the front door.

'Thank you, Mr Theros,' said John.

'We'll be back, I'll guarantee,' added Oscar. 'I'll just drop off my cup.' He headed to the kitchen before I could get them both out the front door.

We stood together for a long moment until Oscar's voice echoed.

'Uh, John, could you bring Theros into the kitchen? There's something you both need to see.'

I froze, hoping it was nothing. Then I heard it, a steady dripping of liquid hitting the table. Unlike paint, blood took time to dry.

Payback
Michael H. Hanson

"But I am faint; my gashes cry for help." – Captain, *MacBeth*, William Shakespeare

Sandy Chu, a twenty-five-year old graduate of the University of Colorado at Boulder, pries open her right eye as best she can with her bruised hands. Blood cakes it and acts like a glue, keeping the lids sealed but she manages to peel them apart. Her left eye has swollen completely shut after the savage beating and is a lost cause. The weird sound and flashing lights that wakened her seem to be getting closer. They are coming from overhead. Perhaps it is a helicopter? Her ears keep ringing and she is pretty sure she has a contusion and probably a cranial fracture. A baseball bat is a hell of a silencer.

The flashing lights shoot over the Flatirons and rapidly move downward over the ten miles that separate them from Sandy's mostly nude form in an open field on the outskirts of Louisville, CO. She keeps losing focus in her right eye and wonders for a moment if she is in the process of dying.

Seconds later the batch of strange lights impact the ground about one hundred yards from her, skidding closer by about seventy-five yards, tearing up dirt and rocks and spewing them in all directions before coming to a stop. The lights die out and under the clear night's moon Sandy can see a rectangular shaped structure half the size of her Bolt electric car. A hatch or door opens on it and something looking like a cross between a ball of seaweed and a spider crawls out and directly toward her.

The shock and pain of Sandy's beating and other atrocities at the hands of those three bastards have left her numb and what might have filled her with terror at any other point in her life now only spurs her curiosity.

So this is how my life ends? She thinks. *Killed or eaten by some monster from outer space?*

The space thing, assuming it is actually an alien from beyond, quickly approaches Sandy and stops mere inches from her face. It smells of salt and decaying flesh. What looks like open wounds bleeding purple gore runs along the rear bulk of the poodle-sized creature. It has five round dark doll-like eyes on a bulbous green forehead. Suddenly, a long ropy appendage emerges from one of two mouths and strikes Sandy's forehead. She immediately blacks out.

***

The night started off innocently enough. After a day of cleaning dishes at Motomaki restaurant, Sandy had driven to her studio apartment in Lafayette, stripped and yanked on t-shirt, shorts and her new Gel-Kayano twenty-sixes and hit the road for a solid run to burn off stress and disappointment.

She stuck to the paved trail and eventually made her way to Louisville. The sun was an hour from dusk and it was a warm summer day with a relaxing breeze. Everything Sandy always liked about an early evening Colorado workout. As the miles flew she pondered her decision to have devoted five years toward a Bachelor of Science degree in Television and Film production. Jobs in this field were at an all-time low in Colorado and she was dreading having to make a decision about relocating to another state, possibly California, to find work. She'd lived her whole life with the southern Rocky Mountains and was loathe to leave them.

The walk/bike path took a sharp turn to the right and, jogging around some thick trees Sandy saw three large men lounging by a van they'd possibly driven along the nearby dirt utility road to this semi-remote location. As she drew closer, Sandy recognized them. The handsome dark bearded man was her new car insurance agent, Frank. In fact, she remembered talking to him a week back about how great the exercise trails were in Boulder County. Next to Frank was a cute young guy with long blonde hair but clean shaven. Dan something or other. A checkout clerk at Alfalfa's Grocery Store she'd talked with a couple of times. The third man was a middle-age African-American fella by the name of Bob, a big friendly mechanic who'd fixed a flat tire for Sandy not two weeks ago.

When she got within ten feet of the guys, who looked like they were just passing the time and shooting the bull, drinking bottles of some dark ale and smoking cigarettes, she slowed to a walk. It was her first and last mistake.

***

Something isn't right. Sandy opens her eyes and gasps. She is standing on a grey flat plain stretching out in every direction for what seems like miles... with no end in sight. The sky is grey with no sun or moon, yet everything is lit around her, as if it is late dusk or early morning. She looks down and wraps her arms around herself. She is naked, but unhurt. She runs her hands over her face and confirms the bruising, cuts and swelling have gone. Her hands feel fine. The nails she had torn off unsuccessfully fighting her three attackers have magically healed. For a moment she brushes her right hand over her lower belly, between her legs. The trauma down there seems to have disappeared, though the memory of it makes her intestines contract.

"Don't tell me this is the afterlife," Sandy says aloud.

No, a voice speaks from behind her, *though my species does not believe in alternate realities or dimensions, I do find your thoughts on them fascinating.*

Sandy spins around and finds herself facing a weird duplicate of herself. Weird because this doppelganger is as pale as an albino, with hair, eyebrows and all of each eye pure white.

"I'm dreaming."

This is not a dream, Sandy, the duplicate speaks in what Sandy realizes is her own voice. *You and I are sharing a temporary looped neural pathway within your brain. This is an artificially created mental construct that allows us to communicate in this manner.*

"Who... what are you?"

I am the severely wounded seaweed spider monster you saw crawl from an alien spaceship and attach a neural-pseudopod to your forebrain. My identification is not something that translates from my race's method of thinking to yours. But for purposes of discussion, you may call me Lom. Now, I have a proposition to make, Sandy.

Sandy backs up a step.

Relax, Sandy, Lom says, *I'm not really here. I'm in your mind. I'm a mental image. Technically you are unconscious. Now be calm, take a few deep imaginary breaths and hear me out. Both of our lives depend on it.*

If this is a dying dream, it's a hell of an interesting one. Sandy nods and does her best to remain calm.

"So what are you proposing?"

Both of our bodies are dying, but my own is in far worse shape than yours. I cannot be repaired. The damage is much too severe. It is, however, within my abilities, my power if you will, to save you and heal all your wounds...

"Yeah?" Sandy says, "well, great. Go for it."

The situation is not that simple. The... let's call it a procedure, requires that I drain my own Connectome-sac and transport all of my cerebral triple-protein-chains into your cerebellum. There is no guarantee that this process will be successful, but if it is, we will both survive, in a manner of speaking....

"What the hell do you mean in a manner?"

My body is dying, it cannot be saved, but, my mind... it can endure... sharing your brain.

"You want to eat my brain," Sandy gasps. "You're a monster!"

Sandy takes two steps back, but Lom just stands there staring at her.

If it were my intention of taking you over, Lom says, *I would have done so already. My species has unbreakable ethical protocols when it comes to these matters. I would die before committing such a heinous act.*

"So, what are you saying?"

You must openly and honestly accept my offer. If there is any resistance in you during this process it will surely fail and we will both die.

"So, we'll like, share my body?"

Yes. Either of us will be able to control it, but only one at a time of course, so we will have to come to immediate accommodations about our future purpose and, what is that concept in your mind, careers.

"This is all so crazy... but you can heal me completely?"

And much more, Lom says, *it is within my abilities to enhance your current physiology far beyond your genome's current capabilities.*

"Like how?"

Lom shows her in a massive series of fabricated images that Sandy witnesses and comprehends in less than a second.

"Why," Sandy mumbles, "I could... I could..."

I can see the dark desires in your mind.

"Do you know what they did to me!" Sandy screams.

Very well. I will save your life and assist you in your mission. But there is a price for this bargain.

"Name it," Sandy says, full of anger.

Lom states her terms. Without hesitation Sandy steps forward and extends her right hand and clasps Lom's duplicate white hand. A moment later their hands begin to fuse together. Seconds later their two forms merge into one. Then there is a blinding explosion of light.

***

Bob Malby spends about two minutes scrubbing the oily grit and grime off his hands with a healthy dose of pumice-laced Gojo in the employee unisex restroom. The Ford dealership closed twenty minutes earlier and he is the lucky employee locking up shop for the night. He turns off the lights in the front offices and locks all the doors before heading back to the service department. He shuts off the computers and lights and then hears a loud clanging noise coming from the service and repair bay.

He walks in and notices the lights are on. He'd shut them off ten minutes ago.

"Who the hell is here! I'm locking up, dammit."

"Hi Bob," a happy voice speaks from behind him.

He spins around and his jaw drops. Standing not twenty feet away from him is that hot chick,

Sandy something or other that his buddies Frank and Dan had invited him to have a night of fun with yesterday. And that's what all three of them had, lots of fun, but making real sure to wear love-gloves and clean the body and surrounding area so nothing could be traced back to them. And Bob knew they'd left just a body because he was the one who had bashed the bitch's skull in with his precious Louisville Slugger autographed by David Ortiz himself. And damn, here she is looking as healthy as a horse. She is an athlete, he remembers that, but now she practically glows with health and damn he can swear that if anything she somehow looks a few inches taller now, with more muscles in her legs and arms.

"Cat got your tongue, mister?" Sandy smirks, taking a step forward.

Bob stands his ground and frowns. Maybe she is a twin.

"Oh, it's me alright, Bob," Sandy chuckles as if she can read his mind and takes another step forward, "I'm the girl you and your bros had a bit too much fun with last night."

"But... how..." Bob mumbles, warily eyeing this preternaturally calm woman dressed in a runner's shirt and shorts and sneakers, "and don't tell me you're a ghost 'cos I don't believe in that shit."

Sandy strides forward, stops right in front of the startled mechanic. She moved so quickly!

"Does this feel like a ghost?" Sandy asks, slapping her right palm roughly on his chest. She is looking at him eye to eye and only wearing sneakers. Bob is a solid six foot three and weighs two hundred twenty-five pounds and none of it fat, but he's beginning to get a weird vibe off this chick. How did she get so damn tall in one day? He grabs her wrist roughly with one large hand and starts to yank it away from him. Then it stops moving.

"What the fu…" Sandy pulls her wrist from his grip then slams her palm forward against his chest, knocking him off his feet and flying backwards for five yards before striking the ground and sliding another two yards, finally stopping at the base of the tire rack.

"It's payback time, Bobby," Sandy says, smiling and moving toward him slowly, "and I'm a girl that likes to collect bills."

Bobby stands up, shaky, and snarls. "You just screwed with the wrong Marine, sugar britches." He takes two strides to the left and removes his precious Louisville Slugger from its wall-mounted trophy rack. He then walks directly at her, the bat rising in both hands like a Samurai sword.

"I don't know what kind of hoodoo you got working for you, slit," he says, getting closer, "but I aim to pound it right out."

With a mighty shrug Bob swings the bat from behind and over his head, the end closing rapidly with Sandy's face. Sandy brings up her right hand and casually catches the bat head in her palm and stops it like a brick wall.

"My turn," she says, then yanks the bat from his hands, slams it against her right knee with her own two hands and breaks it in half.

"How..." Bob starts and then Sandy shoves the sharp splintered base of the bat up through his neck and into his skull. Both his eyes pop out and hang down on his face by their retinas as blood spills from his mouth. Only a gurgling sound is heard as his body sways and convulses.

"Yeah," Sandy says, tossing the other half of the bat away, "you weren't that articulate yesterday either."

***

Dan Harmony, looking like a poster boy for surfer anonymous in his Baja Rules t-shirt, surfer trunks and sandals, leaves the grocery store from the loading dock, having just locked up the place.

Right after passing the Mack truck that won't be taken out until tomorrow morning he stops in his tracks. A woman is standing ten feet away, dressed in running clothes and leaning against a brick wall directly under a security light. And she looks familiar... way too familiar.

"Long time no see, sailor,' Sandy says playfully. "Looking for a good time?"

"Uh, no," Dan mumbles, "maybe some other time."

It's the girl they all had yesterday. He knows it. But it's impossible. She's dead. She has to be. Bob cracked her skull like a melon with that damned baseball bat. Could this be her sister?

"Oh I'm the real thing, Danny," Sandy says with some humor in her voice. "As real as rain and pain. And that look on your face. I'm hurt. Aren't you glad to see me?"

Dan moves forward in an attempt to walk around her but she leaps away from the wall, a full ten feet into the air to quickly land in the middle of the loading dock driveway and block his path of escape. Dan's eyes open wide. This is insane. It's definitely the young woman he and the others had jumped last night. But she's different, somehow bigger than before.

"Bob sends his regards, Danny," Sandy smiles, "but I'm sad to say he didn't make the cut."

"What do you want?"

"I want to dance," Sandy says, walking forward slowly, "and you look like a young man who stays in shape. Nordic Track? Free weights?"

"Third degree black belt in Hapkido."

"Then this should be fun," Sandy snarls and runs right at him.

Without hesitating Dan reaches around with his right hand, shoves it under his long shirt, whips out his Glock Forty-Two and fires four rounds center mass.

The force of the impacts stop Sandy in her tracks… but she doesn't fall.

Dan stands there, about five feet separating them, his body locked in the Chapman Stance, his strong-arm fully extended. There is no blood and he can clearly see she isn't wearing any body armor. What the hell!

Sandy's head is tilted down and it suddenly snaps back up. She smiles an evil smile. "You might say, Danny boy, that I've become a heartless bitch."

Dan fires the remaining three rounds at point-blank range and suddenly makes a quick step to his right at the same time Sandy's right fist shoots forward to move through the space his head has just occupied, as if he somehow anticipates her maneuver.

Without hesitating Dan reverses his grip on his Glock and slams it down and against Sandy's left temple with all of the force and skill at his command. The effect is immediate as the pistol breaks into several pieces that fall to the floor.

"Little bit of an upgrade, Dan," Sandy says with a smile. "My skull now has the density and tensile strength of a single carbon nanotube infested diamond."

Dan swivels into a defensive Hapkido stance.

"You know, Dan," Sandy says, "I've just decided there is one thing more appropriate than death for that wonderfully conditioned body of yours…"

"What?" he asks, his eyes two narrow slits.

"This."

As quick as thought Sandy drops forward onto her right knee and slams a hammer fist strike against Dan's left knee, instantly shattering it. Dan screams, but somehow keeps his balance on his right leg before dropping forward with a well-aimed right elbow strike almost connecting with Sandy's left clavicle. Thrusting up her left elbow, she strikes Dan's, instantly fracturing it. Screaming again and still somehow keeping his balance, Dan rotates his shoulders and commences a left-handed spear finger strike at her eyes. She blocks it with a lazy slap and shoves Dan onto his back on the pavement.

"Dem bones, dem bones gonna bounce around," Sandy sings as she shatters Dan's right knee with a stomp kick. "Dem bones, dem bones gonna jounce about." Next she fractures his left hip with a forward leaning roundhouse punch.

With each strike Dan screams aloud in agony.

"Now feel the might of the lord!" she continues singing, going to work on his ribs and systematically completely permanently crippling him by breaking most of the bones in his body.

***

Frank Ableman, still wearing his black Banana Republic Italian wool suit from the office, walks out of Murdock's Tap & Tavern and gets into his well-maintained first-generation Hummer, starts it up, revs the engine and barrels down South Boulder Road. The bar just closed and Frank knows for a fact that at his time of night there aren't any cops on patrol in a ten mile radius. County cutbacks have left the poor bastards understaffed for the night shift.

He gets up to sixty miles per hour when a quick look at his rearview mirror makes his blood freeze.

"What in Christ's name…"

About one hundred and fifty feet behind him and very slowly catching up, is a woman in a track outfit running like a demon. Frank glances at his speedometer. It clearly shows sixty. This is really happening.

When the running woman closes to within twenty-five feet of his SUV his face contorts. It is that uppity princess he and the boys taught a lesson yesterday. It's night but the streetlamps bordering the road are quite bright and hers is a face he'll never forget. A gorgeous Asian-American chick with a long red stripe through her black hair, sporting deliciously pale green eyes and a heartbreaking grin. Frank remembers the first day Sandy had walked into the insurance office. He knew he just had to have her. It didn't take long, though, for him to see she wasn't interested in a guy ten years older than her and a married one at that. So, he and his buddies decided to give this stuck-up cunt the ride of her life. But they had left her dead. This just isn't possible.

She closes the distance another ten feet and Frank pushes it up to seventy. He glances at the driver's side mirrorand shakes his head. She doesn't even look winded, more like a long-distance runner on pace and not a sprinter giving it their all. He himself had done cross country and track in high school, but that was sixteen years ago and he knew that what she is doing is downright impossible. It is as if Wonder Woman has jumped off the big screen and into the real world and he's some kind of super-villain on the lamb.

On closer examination Frank can see that she seems taller and more muscular than she had yesterday... or perhaps it is a trick of the night, with the streetlamp light flickering on and off. But no matter, she next closes to within ten feet of his rear bumper. He pushes it to eighty as a terrible grin cuts across her face.

The newly installed proximity sensors kick off an alarm warning when Sandy approaches to within six feet of the left back bumper.

Frank reaches and crosses the invisible line separating Louisville from Boulder, makes a quick calculation and readies himself. Sandy, or whatever it is that looks like her, is within a couple of feet of his car and reaching out with her left hand.

When he's a tenth of a mile from crossing Cherryvale Road, he jerks the steering wheel to the right and bursts off of South Boulder Road just as Sandy rips the rear bumper off the car with a swipe of her hand.

The car bounced furiously on the dirt and grass of the open field and slowed down to sixty-five miles per hour. Frank spins the wheel and furiously squints into the night through his driver side window. Sandy was clipped by the back of the truck, knocked over and skidded fifty feet in a long tumble. He sees her stand up and begin to run after him as if she had merely stumbled. It appears that whatever the hell she has become could withstand a great deal of trauma.

Frank knows he desperately needs to even the odds on this playing field and shoves the accelerator to the floor. It is a struggle to keep from flipping the vehicle, but he manages to make it to Cherryvale Road, forcing his precious Hummer to go as fast as it can. A glance at the rearview mirror shows Sandy is twenty-five yards behind and closing.

Thirty seconds later his final destination comes into view.

A crazy ploy jumps into Frank's mind.

What the hell, he thinks, *what's life without a little fun?*

He breaks through the locked gate and barrels directly to the edge of the Baseline Reservoir thirty yards away. A glance shows Sandy has closed the distance and will be on him in fifteen seconds at most. Another quick calculation tells him to push it up to seventy and pray.

Sandy puts on a final sprint. This latest burst of speed is too much for her sneakers, which instantly shred into dozens of pieces which fly off her feet. She closes the distance separating them to ten feet. The reservoir is fifty feet away.

Frank slams on the brakes.

The rest happens in less than a second.

The Hummer smears rubber across thirty plus feet of parking lot, the Hummer rapidly decelerates, so fast that when it gets to within twenty feet of the water Sandy collides with it, bounces upward and over the car and strikes the water a full fifteen feet out. Frank brings the truck to a full stop about ten feet from water's edge when he slams his foot on the gas, jumps forward and toward a dazed Sandy who is standing neck high in warm water. By the time she realizes what's happening it's too late. The natural buoyancy of the Hummer and its weight and forward momentum carry it out to impact her, knocking her a foot under water.

Frank quickly opens all the doors, allows the vehicle to fill with water and rapidly sink, pinning Sandy underneath.

After quickly settling down. the truck lifts upwards incrementally twice. Frank realizes that as strong as this nightmare appears to be, leverage is a major problem when lying on her back. He jumps out of the Hummer after opening the doors and walks to within a few feet of where she is pinned. The water is up to his neck, but the nearest reservoir lamp shines clearly through the relatively clean liquid, even this close to midnight. Sandy is struggling but to no avail. She stops moving when she notices Frank looking down at her, his face almost touching the surface of the water.

"I don't know if you can hear me, sweetmeat," Frank sneers, "but before you drown, I just wanted you to know that you were the tightest and juiciest piece of snatch I ever slammed."

Frank grins then turns back to shore, only to realize his right foot is stuck on something.

"What the…" he starts saying when he is savagely yanked underwater.

In a moment he's face to face with the woman he raped and tortured to death the day before. Her lower body is pinned under the front left tire. Her lips move and Frank realizes that he can hear her clearly, regardless of the water that surrounds them both.

"Something tells me, Frankie, that none of your insurance policies will cover this contingency."

Frank panics and struggles, but to no avail. His breath fails after a full minute and, as water cascades into his mouth and nose as he convulses, Sandy chuckles.

***

Sandy stands on the shore of the reservoir and ponders the summer stars overhead.

"That was a neat trick, Lom. Inflating my torso to the point that we could push the Hummer off of us."

Glad to be of help, Lom replies in her head, *even though we could have survived for several weeks in an all-water environment, I generally prefer unencumbering planetary atmospheres to preside in.*

"And you think it will only take a couple of weeks to repair your starship?" Sandy asks.

Yes, Lom replies, *maybe less and then we can finish my own pressing mission, which was so unceremoniously interrupted by that surprise meteor shower responsible for forcing me onto your planet.*

"Will I be lonely in outer space?" Sandy asks.

There are thousands of intelligent races spread throughout the galaxy, Lom says, *and quite a few different humanoid species not unlike you Terrans. I think you will find this to be a wonderful and exciting adventure, Sandy. One which no human has ever experienced before.*

"Do you think we'll have time to ever come back to Earth... for a visit?"

Your concept of time is an odd one, Sandy, Lom replies. B*arring overwhelming catastrophe or* *intentional murder, I can renew the cells of our body for tens of thousands of what you call years.*

"Lom," Sandy says, "this looks like the beginning of a beautiful friendship."

When They Come for You
Rie Sheridan Rose

When they come for you,
it will be too late
to call "Do over!"
or attempt to hide.

When they come for you,
all your wicked deeds
will come home to roost
on the ashes that remain.

When they come for you,
you may bargain
or plead, but it
will be in vain.

They do not care why
you did those things you did.
The demons only know their
master wants your soul.

Tragic Lullaby
Jim Dyar

Leaves were leaping underfoot in a bitter wind blowing down Willow Street. Paul braced himself against the cold. He hated taking this route, but it cut fifteen minutes off his walk home after practice.

He huddled down into his coat, becoming aware of a stray melody reaching him from upwind. Charmed by it, he followed until he spotted the tree the street was named after, a huge weeping willow anchored firmly inside the gates of Everton Cemetery.

Paul was unable to ignore the song, so he slipped past the gate and made his way to a single mausoleum where the music seemed to be emanating from.

On the stone before him, half-revealed by a nearby streetlight, was a series of notes. They were moving into and out of his field of vision which should have concerned him. Instead, it gave the impression that such a strangely built tomb was created to be a musical; box.

He stared in the semi-darkness, listening hard. He could detect a girl's voice somewhere amongst the ethereal instrumental, all perfectly balanced and harmonized. He struggled to pick the words out of the enchanted melody, but failed to even grasp the point of the song.

Then suddenly a gasp and it stopped.

Paul jolted as if from a trance.

"No. Wait."

There was no more noise, just an expectant silence.

"Please. It was so beautiful."

Paul waited in anguish. Had he ruined it by interfering? Had he somehow insulted the musician?

Eventually a tiny voice spoke from a place where no one seemed to be.

"It's a song of ruin," said a melodic female voice. "I wrote it, then it destroyed me."

Paul shook his head.

"I can't imagine anything so beautiful causing sadness."

When the voice spoke again, it seemed to be flattered.

"You take your fate in your hands this night if you ask me to play it again."

Paul settled on the dirt and leaned forward eagerly.

"Please."

The song began again. It was strangely moving, very ghostly. It almost seemed to caress him in the night. He lost all track of time, only returning to his parent's house at the first light of dawn.

***

Paul never forgot that night.

He turned to the newly formed computer industry where he made his first million, then got married and had kids. Paul lived the dream until the market crashed, leaving him penniless. The disaster helped him learn friends and family meant nothing as one by one they abandoned him.

Paul's fiftieth birthday came and passed in a cardboard box. Hunger and disease had cost him an eye and his ability to walk far. It was almost too much to make his way to the soup kitchen for food.

He sat there staring out into the street until he heard a tiny ghostly whisper.

"Was it worth it?"

Paul simply smiled.

"Yes, it was,"

Paul got the impression the voice was pleased.

The song played again, stronger than before. The music lifted his soul from the decrepit earth and carried him home.

Can You Not Smell Them?
Dona Fox

The broken lock was still in motion. The aroma of Bettie's French toast drifted into the hallway through cracks in the shattered door and should have comforted me but it didn't. I was sure Bo Chance had passed through this doorway just before I arrived. In fact, I was certain of it.

Bo's adrenaline-tinged sweat hung in the air. I was afraid enough of him but there was also a stranger's scent telling me Bo had not been alone.

I pressed against the oily wallpaper as I slid back into the darkness of the hall, away from the murky window, out from under the fly-specked lightbulb. I listened for sounds from inside Old Bettie's apartment. I waited for her screams—then would I race to help?

If I saw fleeing figures run through the door, past the broken lock, how long would I wait to enter, long enough for a heart to stop? Or would I slink back down the urine-soaked stairwell pretending I'd never arrived?

Bo and I were young and homeless. We were part of a hard group that ran a bunch of grifts, cons—whatever scams our marks were ripe for us to employ. Fast in, fast out—that was our motto. Mostly we were pick-pockets.

I'd met Old Bettie over beers in Ginny's Bar. We shared smokes in the alley and become fast friends while we formed the usual smokers' bond.

The old woman's social security check never got her through the month. I had food stamps but nowhere to cook.

Old Bettie took the stamps and said she'd cook for the two of us. What did I like? *French Toast.* Beneath blunt white bangs and thick lenses, her pale freckled lips had stretched into a smile. *One of my specialties.*

The old woman lived in a chill, narrow apartment in the collapsing Mallory Arms across the alley from Ginny's Bar. She said it was one of the 'luxury' apartments as she had two burners and a tiny fridge. A scratchy army blanket covered the mattress on her twin bed and the pillow was flat and uncased. Beside the bed there was a small table and one wobbly chair. She said she'd traded the useless extravagance of a closet for a window that looked down on a vacant lot.

I never went straight from the last place, I grifted to Ginny's Bar or directly from the bar to the Mallory.

She had an old smoker's cough–always followed by a chuckle. Then, with a twinkle in her eye–like a tunnel to the past,–Old Bettie told me some wild tales; said she'd been a cook in a logging camp in the rough timber of the Pacific Northwest. Even though I'd come to think of her as my granny I only half believed her stories and often wondered if she'd picked up the accounts listening to loggers who'd passed through the bar and not from her own experience, albeit I'd known no such men to frequent Ginny's in my time.

One night she pulled a ragged envelope out from between the striped mattress and the rusty springs of her bed and showed me money she'd stashed away. A lot of money. *If anything happens to me this is yours, you take it. Don't share it with that boy. You hear me, Sahara? I mean it just for you.* Her trust in me, a pick-pocket, made my nose swell.

Then she had me pull two dusty shoeboxes out from under the bed. If they held more secrets, she was taking too long about it. Once I'd seen the money, I was sure Bo would be here soon—he could smell that much green ink in a skunk's grave.

I kept watching the door, listening for his footsteps. Sure, he was my partner, my sometimes lover, but we were grifters; I expected nothing but thievery from him.

One shoebox was empty but for a blue-black weapon, her gun. Bettie sat on the bed, the gun forgotten on her lap as she opened the other box. She pulled out letters tied with pink ribbons and pictures of herself, young and beaming, standing next to tall, burly, bearded men.

Bettie ran a rippled nail across a fading face. *This one said he'd always be watching over me.*

He had the wood folk's special ken about him, told them they'd gone too deep into the forest. The roots of the ancient trees were stirring. He said to the bosses—Can you not smell their anger on the wind? But his bosses pushed him and I believe because he had the sight and yet went on—they came for him.

Couple days later a fallen tree fish-tailed as it swept across a clearing, swung sideways and took him out. She talked until she lost her voice and I fell asleep, belly full of her warm buttery, eggy, syrupy French toast.

The next day I came upon the open door, the broken lock–I'm ashamed I took so long to push the thin door open and go into the tiny apartment. The old woman wasn't there. A torn shoebox was lying on the lumpy bed, empty. Bo must have the gun.

I'm even more ashamed that I picked up the warm French Toast already congealing in the butter on the blackened skillet before I ran out the door with the box of memories that might help me find her.

But I didn't need the letters and photos; she was sprawled in the rear stairwell. Dead. I went back to her apartment and slipped my hand between the mattress and the springs; the envelope was there—odd. Why hadn't Bo sensed the presence of the cash? I hid the money on me with the skill of a practiced pick-pocket. Then I called emergency.

Days later I sat in the taxi clutching a different cardboard box. My heart pounded through my body; shock-waves vibrated clear down to my hands and left sweaty crescents–guilty fingerprints on the carton. Old Bettie was in there, or rather her cremains.

I'd made arrangements to place her in a vault at a nearby mortuary. They were expecting me that afternoon. I was putting her money to good use–the taxi, the mortuary, I would even rent her apartment and keep it as a shrine.

Stunning how quickly they'd torched her after identification, there being no 'unusual circumstances' surrounding her death–they thought she was a confused old woman and she'd simply fallen–along with the fact that I was there to identify her.

When I left the crematorium on Duncan, Bo was waiting for me. I wouldn't show him any fear; I held my head up high.

"What's going on, Sara?" He squinted at me as he took a pinchy drag from his cigarette.

I shuddered for the zillionth time at the butchering of my name. I was Sahara, not Sara. Old Bettie had always called me Sahara.

Bo bent over, put his face directly in front of mine and raised his voice, "I said what's going on?"

I fought to remain calm. "Old Bettie had insurance for a vault at the mortuary on Main Street. And the transport of her remains.–this taxi." I lied as I waved my hand at the car that pulled up.

"Oh." He tossed his still-burning cigarette into the road and pushed himself into the taxi beside me.

The sun was shining but as our car proceeded down Duncan to Main Street, the sky filled with gray clouds and the day turned dark then the rain began.

Small branches flew as the winds picked up. Rain beat against the cab; dark-winged wipers flew uselessly across the window. I focused on the sound of the wet street being shushed by the tires; with eyes closed I could measure the slight progression as the tires threw more water up beside the car until it sounded as if the cab was skimming over waves.

Then the cabbie's radio squawked. He spoke, the radio squawked again, and then he pulled over.

"I can't go any farther. There's a wire down across Main." He sat there, the meter running.

Bo grabbed the back of the front seat and barked into the cabbie's ear, "what are we supposed to do? Walk?" as if by threatening him he could change the man's orders.

The cabbie straightened in his seat and continued to look out the front window, "if you wish."

I begged him to turn the cab around and take us and Old Bettie's cremains to her apartment. The sun came out again as we climbed the steps.

"You don't need to babysit me, Bo."

"You shouldn't be alone with your friend's ashes."

I couldn't get rid of him. He smelled the money.

The next day was sunny and clear. I was going to the mortuary and once again called a taxi.

Bo insisted on waiting outside with me. Before the taxi arrived at Old Bettie's apartment, another–even worse–storm struck.

"That damn taxi should be here. Making us wait in this weather–you don't tip him, understand?"

"Sure, Bo."

The taxi never arrived. I tried to open the door to go back inside the Mallory but Old Bettie's card wouldn't work and the touchpad was out of order. We'd have to wait for someone who was leaving the building to let us in.

"I'll be at Ginny's. Come get me." So much for not leaving me alone with my friend's ashes.

Bo left–for a beer or to meet the stranger? I hadn't forgotten the other scent, the smell of another entity, strange to me–someone or something else who had been with Bo in Bettie's apartment on the day that she died. Or someone had murdered her.

I was standing on the covered porch when I heard my name, "Sahara," and someone tapped me on the shoulder.

"What?" I turned but no one was there.

"It was Bo and something more violent."

I looked through the rain, searching for the source of the voice and saw a small stand of trees in the vacant lot on the other side of the Mallory from Ginny's Bar. I heard shouts, saw dancing lights, and figures moving about. Perhaps someone who could let me into the building so I could dry off, have a warm cup of coffee, and stop these hallucinations of conscience.

As I entered the grove, I heard children laughing which gave me courage and I pressed on, even when I saw the markers–the crosses, the headstones. I'd entered a graveyard. I'd never noticed a graveyard here–but then I'd never been looking for a graveyard so of course I hadn't noticed it.

Had I come upon a burial in progress? What about the flickering lights I'd seen earlier–did the mourners have candles? Even in this storm?

Now I could see no people, yet the sound of shovels scraping against the rocky soil chilled my spine and set my teeth on edge. My sodden coat still guarded the box of cremains. Water poured down my scalp and ran across my face. In the constant barrage of lightning, I looked around me.

The place was indeed a graveyard, but one long abandoned. No one tended this place. Wild bushes had claimed the center and weeds covered the broken markers. Someone had sprayed the fallen stones with graffiti. Bottles and cans littered the ground along with other debris that made this land look like the high tide line of the ocean.

Did the debris and graffiti signal this was a meeting place for rebellious teens? Perhaps a gang waited to harm me? Not in this storm. I jumped as a loud crack echoed behind me. A branch fell to the ground with a soft thud. I looked up into the trees. Would there be more? Was I safe or would a falling tree also take me out?

Old Bettie burned hot against my stomach. Perhaps if I laid her to rest the storms would calm and the violence would draw back from around me. As the icy rain pelted my face the wind whipped my hair into the air and tore at my coat. I dropped to my knees and dug into the muddy earth with my fingernails.

Now the voices were murmuring. I felt like a prickly cat; each whisper a stranger stroking my back.

I patted the last bit of ground over the hasty grave, then I saw her.

She glowed in all colors and yet none. As I stared, she spoke, "Stay here. Wait with me. Bo is inside plotting with the stranger."

She indicated the Mallory. I looked up and saw Bo in the window, watching us.

The ominous presence that shadowed him like a dark halo was compelling, "I should go in," with a last pat on Old Bettie's grave, I rose on trembling legs.

"Go in and you'll die. He knows about the money. He'll kill you for it."

I didn't know what to do. I felt I owed Old Bettie but I'd buried her. What more could I do out here?

"Stay with me longer," the cold ground sent up a warm pull that enveloped me. I could have leaned back into it, closed my eyes and felt safe. Stayed there forever, died there. A soft death. A gentle death.

But as I looked up at the window, a grim-faced Bo was waving at me, demanding that I come in.

"Please stay, Sahara." Old Bettie urged me,–so I stayed, but I had a plan. I positioned myself so that I was standing next to and facing Bettie's grave.

Bo disappeared from the window. In a few moments he came stomping into the graveyard. I could see the outline of the gun beneath his clothes. He kept tugging at the hem of his shirt with one hand and his other hand fidgeted, eager to get to the weapon–to pull it out and use it.

He came charging up to me and, as I knew he would, he stood right in front of me, and put his face in mine, threatening, bullying, "Didn't you see me, Sara? Why wouldn't you come inside?" he looked around, once, twice, then back at me; "did you bury her? Are you finished?"

"Yes, she's right there, in fact you're standing on her."

"No." and as he looked down at his feet Old Bettie's grave shifted, opened. Then the ground beneath him turned red, his shoes melted and he sank into the earth; "what the hell is happening?" he demanded as if, once again, being a bully would be enough. As if he could intimidate the very Earth.

Then the darkness swooped down on him from above, and his wicked friend took the form of a vulture and wrapped its wings around Bo and attempted to draw him back from the earth that threatened to devour him. I watched Bo's body tremble, shake, and then he radiated so much heat that the edges of the wings that held him flared crimson before they too turned to ash.

I had to step back and turn my face away, but from the tenor of his screams I was certain he was no longer a threat.

When the air cooled enough for me to turn back, it appeared he hadn't melted down into Old Bettie's grave after all. Instead he seemed to be rejuvenated; he'd popped up next to her grave with a big smile on his face.

He said, "I could use some French Toast. Sahara, how about you? It's my specialty."

And I swear he cast two shadows—one very short, the other tall and gangly—and his shadows seemed to hold each other's hands as he turned and walked back to the Mallory.

Just a Woman
Frances Gow

Jade steps off the tube at Tottenham Court Road station. The doors racket shut behind her and she turns to watch the train jerk into motion before it thunders into the antiquated tunnel. She rocks on her heels, unbalanced by the turbulence of the departing train. Her left arm dangles at her side, covered only by an over-sized raincoat that droops over her body. The platform stretches out before her and she moves forward to study the tracks, tantalisingly close to the edge. People scurry towards the exits like iron filings drawn towards a magnet.

Need somewhere... just to hang out for a couple of hours. She turns, her pulse quickening with every stride she takes, yet her legs move as though they are filled with lead. For all she knows, they could be just ahead of her. Despite this, she worries about keeping the doctor waiting too long; it was hard enough to find someone willing to complete the surgery.

Her heels click-clack down the endless stretch of tunnel tarmac and all she wishes is to kick off the cursed shoes and run. People stare at her dishevelled state; torn shirt, coat pocket ripped to shreds, smeared make-up and very likely stale perfume. She knows what people are thinking. A bust up with her partner and a night on the streets would have been a fair assumption. Her stomach lurches with every glance from a stranger.

They could be anywhere.

There is no one she can trust.

She tries in vain to cover herself with the raincoat and only succeeds in drawing attention to the lifeless limb at her side.

Jade is desperate to sit down, to put the world on hold for five minutes but hardly dares stop. Must keep moving... must get away. The escalator rumbles ahead and she steps on, turning herself away from onlookers travelling in the opposite direction. A long fringe of strawberry-blonde hair flops across her face obscuring the wretchedness of her expression. She is haunted by shadows, looking over her shoulder and finally steps out into the bitter afternoon chill, hurrying down the street towards Holborn.

The crowd dissipates as she walks farther away from the station. There is a place she knows where once she would sit and drink coffee before work, in the days before her career really took off. Office administrator to sales director in only ten years. It had been hard, but she needed the money to pay for the alterations that would eventually buy her freedom.

Holborn station looms up ahead and Jade turns right into Kingsway and strides away from the crowds milling around on the corner.

She glances right and left before stepping into the Italian cafe, hoping that the proprietor does not recognise her. The smell of fresh coffee and chocolate awakens nostalgia for long lunches in the company of friends, easing the tension in her body.

"Cappuccino please," she whispers. The man barely glances at her as he grunts and nods his head towards the booths. She slides into the nearest one and sinks into the comfort of the padded seat. Somewhere she can sit, alone, without drawing attention to herself. A passer-by would not notice her there.

She lifts the coat to inspect her arm. It is numb. A blue tinge colours her skin and a tingle runs down her left side as the drug begins to diffuse.

She jumps as a coffee cup drops onto the table in front of her, white froth spilling down its sides. The waitress scribbles onto a piece of paper and slips it under the saucer, her eyes flicking towards the mark on Jade's cheek. Her insides tighten for a moment before the waitress turns to attend to another table. She rearranges her hair to hide the scar; an unsightly reminder of a tattoo she once tried to have removed.

They had come for her. After so many years of hiding and working to earn the money for a new life, a new identity. As long as she was just a woman, there was no telling who or what she had once been. She had earned her stake in this life and once she reached that four o'clock appointment in Harley Street, she fully intended to realise that. And yet, with only hours to pass before that final appointment, they had come.

She sips the coffee and licks sweet chocolate from her lips. Her arm tingles, twitches and relief floods her. The drug is starting to wear off. A little girl watches her from over the top of the adjoining booth, oval brown eyes stare in wonder at the woman with the haunted look. Jade smiles, then looks away, feeling uncomfortable under the gaze of the child. The mother chides.

"Mica ,don't stare, it's rude." The little face disappears. A man enters. Out of earshot, he speaks to the owner then takes a seat within sight of Jade's booth. He pulls out a newspaper, crosses one leg over the other and begins to read. The paper moves to one side and he catches her eye, lingers for an instant then resumes reading. Jade's heart pounds and the blood rushes round her head.

What if he is one of them?

Who is to know?

They could be anywhere. Watching, waiting. She glances over her shoulder and sees the owner talking into the telephone... maybe he knows; maybe he is telling them where to find her. She panics and rises, then sits back down, gulping in deep breaths. No, don't draw attention. If she runs, they will know for sure, there is nothing sinister about making a phone call.

"Another one, love?"

Jade's stomach lurches and she looks up at the waitress who reaches for her empty cup. She nods and slumps back into her seat. They would come for sure if she didn't make a move soon. She reached inside her pocket and feeelt for the reassuring cold steel of the pistol that had bought her the time to get this far.

They had been waiting for her in the underground car park. She stepped out of the executive lift and stopped, face to face with an automatic handgun. The thug was working for them. His stubbly chin and unkempt hair enhanced the wild look in his eye. Four more stepped out of the shadows, one a woman. They wore special ID for the entire world to see. Licensed to be thugs. The nausea made her gag. They hadn't even bothered to send the Chief - these were just henchmen, doing dirty work for the government. Bastards.

"Well," the gunman said. His lopsided mouth gave his grin an ugly, menacing effect. On a power trip, thought Jade, revolted by his enjoyment of the moment. He beckoned to one of the other men who moved forward.

"What do you want?" Jade was trying to sound calm but the play dumb method didn't work as the man grabbed her by the neck and smeared a wet cloth across her face. The stench of cleaning fluid rushed into her nostrils. Her cheek stung, tears sprang into her eyes and her nose began to run. They all took a step forward; the man who held her neck took a handful of her hair and pulled, so she had no choice but to look up into the faces peering at their evidence.

"Batch 23," he said. "She tried to have it removed, but there's no mistaking that mark." He pushed her away with disgust.

Another one stepped forward and spat in her face. The woman stood with her arms folded. Her jaws worked a steady rhythm around her chewing gum. She laughed.

Jade howled.

"I'm just a woman," she said and ripped open her shirt to reveal the soft white skin of her body.

"Hardly conclusive," the gunman said. Jade covered herself and stood sobbing. The woman came forward, muscles rippling along her forearms. She looked more of a freak than Jade could have managed even if she'd been trying.

"It's what you have inside that counts," she said as she punched Jade in the stomach. The pain was crushing. The woman took a two-fingered grip on the symbiotic parasite lodged inside her and squeezed. An alien cry of anguish escaped Jade's lips; she could not help herself, it was her nature.

"Batch 23," she said, laughing. She moved her hand away and wiped a film of mucus down her trouser leg. Jade bent over double and the others roared with mirth.

"Ever screwed one of them?" the gunman said.

"You sick bastard," said another.

"I say we shoot its head off."

The woman grabbed a fistful of Jade's hair and pulled her head up, looking into her eyes. Tears of pain streaked down her face and the woman grinned.

"Nah," she said. "Too much money riding on this one, boys." She gave an extra twist, just to emphasise the point. A man with round glasses and thin pointy nose stepped forward and took a large hypo from a case. They brought the medic. Jade watched as he checked the needle and the liquid . She panicked and struggled but the thug with the gun just stepped forward and pressed it to her temple. The woman released her hold and began to free Jade's left arm from her coat.

"You won't kill me," Jade said. "I have information hidden that will expose you all."

"Don't push your luck, honey," the woman said. "Accidents happen." She took a firm hold of Jade's cuff and ripped the sleeve off in one. "You're lucky you managed to survive this long on the outside. The rest of batch 23 was rounded up shortly after the press got the whiff of a story. You're the only one who slipped the net. Just take your medicine like a good girl." The woman sneered and turned the wrist upward so the medic could find a vein. He prodded around until satisfied, then looked up at the gunman. He shook his head and waved the thug back. Jade relaxed a little as the gunman moved to a position some feet away. Then, with an apologetic look, the medic took a pinch of skin and slipped the needle into her arm. She watched in morbid terror as he pushed down on the syringe pump. She closed her eyes.

Shards of light stabbed at the insides of her eyelids as a multitude of images flashed through her mind. The clinical whiteness of the womb of her childhood; surrounded by machinery, experimental embryos. Spewing babies with the systematic regularity of a conveyor belt, discarding the bad nuts, nourishing the survivors. And the pain... it rushed to her head and threatened to split her skull. Medical staff, who bore down on her with dispassionate interest. Nannies from hell, who cared not for the piss and shit of bringing up babies. And then, there was the batch that escaped. Born of no man or woman, being neither; not even human.

Jade opened her eyes slowly. The drug was kicking in, though the syringe was only half-empty. Her head was thumping with the sounds of the empty car park rushing to her eardrums with deafening amplification. Her eyes blurred and focused, blurred and focused. Faces leered at her from all directions and the concrete walls surrounding them turned in and out as though the entire structure was breathing with life. Images and sensations became intensely small and in turn obscenely large as she panted and blew through her mouth while the surrounding area bulged and retracted. She heard the sound of concrete grating and rumbling above her head and looked up as the ceiling descended, layers of concrete slamming towards her. She screamed and wrenched the syringe free of her arm, stabbing it into the chest of the medic. He fell to the floor, trying to wrestle himself free.

Everything stopped.

It was like a veil thrown across the scene, she watched, detached, at the looks of panic that washed over the faces of the thugs in slow waves. Every arm moved towards its chest as she realised that the gunman was not the only one armed. She watched his arm raise and his stance drop in micro slow motion. Before he had a chance to aim, Jade had clasped her own pistol with her free hand and, without taking it out of her pocket, she shot the gunman. He fell, legs splayed. She released her remaining shots before the others managed to extract their guns from their holsters. There was a look of utter bewilderment on their faces as they crumpled to the ground.

Jade stood for a second as her senses calmed and her ears rang with the echo of gunfire. She watched the bodies twitch and the blood pool around her. The medic convulsed in the midst of his own nightmare, clutching the empty syringe to his chest. She had one shot left. She stood over him and watched in fascination as he writhed around on the floor. Let him have a taste of his own medicine. She slipped the gun into her other pocket and ran, the residue scent of metallic gunshot lingering in the air.

A blast of cold air enters the café as the door opens and shuts behind Jade's booth. She sinks in her seat and the waitress gives her an odd look as she deposits another coffee on the table. The little girl is staring at her again and Jade summons the courage to smile a little but the child stares back, expressionless. The crumple of newspaper pages being turned distracts her attention and she glances at the man with the paper. He is staring at something at the front of the café near the counter. Her chest tightens and her breathing becomes shallow and quick. There is someone talking with the proprietor. Footsteps sound, moving in her direction. Now the paper man is looking at her. A suit steps into view and stands in front of her, looking at her wretched state as she cowers into the corner of the seat like a trapped animal. Finally, they had conceded to send someone of rank. The sudden burst of laughter from her lips is bitter and maniacal. The official looks sympathetically at her and this just makes her want to cry with frustration.

"There are two armed response vehicles parked out front and back," he says, releasing a clean hypo from its case. He indicates her left arm and she lets the coat fall away. There is a small gasp and Jade looks up at the little girl who is still watching, her mother oblivious to the events occurring in the booth next door.

"Please," Jade says. "Not in front of the child..."

"Your weapon." He holds out a hand with a kind of gentle faith, which takes her by surprise. She nods and slips her hand into the pocket. She clutches the pistol and realises then that she cannot go back to all the pain and suffering of her past existence. She wants to trust this man, though she knows he is working for them.

Ten years ago, she and her last remaining siblings of batch 23 broke free from their prison. She was the only one who made it. There was really only one way she could ever be truly free.

The government official smiles. He is the only one who has ever shown her any compassion. Perhaps it is all right to trust him. Perhaps he won't let them hurt her any more. He reaches for her hand and she lets him touch her.

"It's okay... really," he says. She pulls her hand out of her pocket with the pistol. She bends over double and groans. The man moves forward almost as a gesture of comfort to his ward and her lips embrace the cold steel barrel in a kiss of death; her final defiant gesture. The man watches in horror as she lifts her head. Blood and tears and the contents of her mind paint the walls of the café with Jade's last will and testament.

Devil's Spawn
Diane Arrelle

Mary dragged the child along the wooded path.

"Come on!" she snapped. "We have to get home before dark. Devil does his work after sundown."

The child whimpered and tried to pull from her grip.

Mary turned, faced the small girl and flinched once again when she saw the mixed breeding in the small heart shaped face. The tainting of the races was a sure sign of the Dark Prince's work. She frowned at the orphan she'd just taken in and thought, *luckily I'm here to save the marked children*. "Come, on, Angela 14, stop fighting. I'm saving you."

The child yanked at the hands that held her and said in a weepy voice, "My mommy named me Melissa."

Mary took in a deep breath, shocked by the defiance this demon's spawn was displaying. She let go of the girl's wrist and smacked her across the face so hard her hand stung. The child staggered backwards then fell and Mary felt satisfaction ease her pained hand. "Your Mommy left you because you're cursed by the Devil. You were born out of wedlock and are doomed to burn in Hell. Now stop that damned crying. I'm going to save your soul!"

Not like that last one. That redheaded spawn had been older and proved to be unsalvageable.

Mary shuddered at the very memory of it. That green fire right outside her house and the Devil himself stealing Angela 13 away. It had shaken her so badly she'd waited a year to find another soul to save.

The sun was setting when they broke through to the small clearing with the shabby cabin in the center. "Here's a bucket, fill it with water in the stream we just passed and don't even think about running away. These woods are full of monsters after dark."

She watched, contempt curling her mouth into a sneer as the girl took the bucket. *All any of them need is some good healthy fear to set them on the road to salvation.* Then she frowned and mumbled, "All except that one with the devil's kiss on her face."

She remembered when she started saving children. The first had been her stepsister Angie. They'd had different fathers, but only Mary's had been a daddy. She'd drowned Angie in the stream when she was eight. Oh how Momma had cried about the accident and prayed for the dead girl's soul.

That was when Mary realized her calling, to save as many souls as she could. A few of her Angelas had run off, but they'd had Satan beaten out of them before they left. She glanced over at the unmarked graves on the edge of the clearing and nodded at the souls she had managed to truly save.

The girl came back, struggling to carry the heavy bucket.

"That's good, Angela 14. Now come here." She stood by a tiny lean-to on the side of the cabin. She grabbed the girl, pushed up the long tattered skirt and snapped a locked chain around the small ankle.

"This is your room. You got a fresh straw bed and a bible."

"But, but, it's dark. I'm scared. Why can't I come in with you?" the child wailed, tears rolling down her cheeks.

"Because I don't let any of the Devil's spawn cross my threshold. Never let the darkness into my home. My soul is clean and I aim to keep it that way."

"Please, I promise to be a good Angela!" Melissa begged, falling to her knees.

Mary snickered, smacked the girl for good measure and turned away. To be blinded by a huge flash of green fire. She stepped back, gasping in terror. That light! Angela 13 had disappeared into that pillar of green fire a year ago.

And now, as her vision returned, there was Angela 13 standing before her, dressed in a rich emerald green gown. She smirked at Mary as she shook back her long, thick, red hair. The birthmark on her cheek was glowing.

"I was right; you are the spawn of the Devil. I saw him take you last year. I watched from the window. Damned! You were damned, unable to be saved!"

"You mean murdered, you murdered those children, not save them," Angela 13 said, her voice dripping with hatred. "But to you murder means salvation. And I'm not the Devil's Spawn. I'm his wife."

The little girl was screaming and the redhead looked at her. "There, there, child. My name is Glory. Come here to me."

She snapped her fingers and the chain dropped to the ground. The little girl ran to her and hugged her waist. "You have your name back, Melissa. You can be my child if you'd like. I promise to love you and care for you until the time comes when no one like her," she pointed at Mary, "will care about the color of your skin or what you believe. Until then, you can stay safe with me and the others I.ve rescued."

Mary was edging away.

Glory stopped her with a commanding stare. Then she smiled sweetly at the woman who had intended to kill her like the others before her. "Mary, my husband and I have decided to repay the favors you have spent your life bestowing on innocent, helpless, young girls, so we have decided to have you live with us as well."

Mary's eyes widened as she watched the handsome man walk out from the flames. He took Glory's hand and kissed the strawberry birthmark on her cheek. "Yes, come join us. You will be known as Angela 15 and we have a special place we made just for you. Right near our home, you know, because we can't have your tainted soul crossing our threshold, can we?"

Mary stood frozen to the spot, unable to respond, unable to get away from the couple facing her, smiling at her. She mouthed the words nonononono but no sound escaped her lips.

Glory kissed her husband back and said to Mary, "Ah, sadly you'll never understand what real evil is, Angela 15. You'll never understand we are not the evil, our duty is to put the evil ones where they belong." She shook her head then turned away and nodded to her husband.

In response, he snapped his fingers and the pillar of fire widened and engulfed Mary. She struggled and inhaled deeply, trying to ward off the flames, but all she could do with her endless last breath was scream and scream with the burning pain that would go on forever.

Sometime in the Small Hours
Gary Budgen

Sometime in the small hours Colin rings. I know it's him, who else would it be? I know what he's going to say.

"When they came for you..." he says as he always does at some point.

"I know," I say, "when they came, you saved me."

"Yes," he says, "I saved you."

We go on talking, mostly about when we were kids, Colin wanting me to tell him that how he remembers it all is how it really happened. We talk about the house of course and at some point I ask him where he is. But Colin won't say. He never does.

***

The house is not far from the rundown estate where the three of us live but a few streets make all the difference. We go just after midnight, across the High Street and a few rows of terraces, then a neighbourhood of fading grand houses. The house on the corner is one of the largest and most impressive even if it could do with a new roof and there's paint flaking on the pillared entrance. Like most of these houses it's set back from the street with a large front drive overgrown enough to provide plenty of places to hide, both from the road and from the house itself.

Not that the woman who lives in the house ever looks out. Marco has told us she lives alone. No visitors apart from deliveries. He's been watching and assured us the whole job will be a piece of cake.

The front door is perfectly shadowed. The lock pathetic.

"Almost an invitation," Marco says.

We enter the hallway. Distant light comes from up the stairs, picking out the clutter of shapes around us, bars at the edge of some sort of cage on a table, picture frames with fancy decorations, the pictures themselves only a massy blackness.

I feel an odd sensation within a few steps as though the floorboard gives a little under my feet. There might be a sound, like a tide coming across sand and bubbling around rocks. But this must be imagination. There is the heavy regular ticking of a clock and a smell not just of dust but something musky, animal.

***

"I knew," says Colin on the phone, "as soon as we went in there was something special about the house. But it wasn't just me, was it? I think if Marco hadn't been there me and you would have just bolted. But we always went along with things to impress him, didn't we?"

"I suppose so."

Marco was a year or so older than us. He'd bragged about break-ins he'd done before. He made it a big thing he was trusting us to help him with this one.

"Sometimes," says Colin, and his voice falls to a whisper, "I imagine I'd left. Sometimes…"

"Are you all right?" I ask.

"It was all for the best in the end though. Yes, yes…"

"Look," I say, "It's late. I have to get up in the morning."

"Oh, your job. Your little job."

Yes, it is pathetic someone my age working in a fast-food joint. Flipping burgers. Grilling chicken. But the regularity, the contact with others, is something I tell myself I need.

"I'm going now, Colin," I say, "take care."

***

Marco nods to a door on the right and turns the handle. The smell inside the room is even stronger. He flicks on his electric torch.

"I've stepped in something," says Colin.

Marco shushes him. The beam of the torch has lit up the floor. There are little piles across the wooden floorboards.

"Cat shit," Marco says, keeping his voice low, "Dirty cow lets her cats shit everywhere."

He moves the torch beam slowly around the room. A settee. An armchair. Walls lined with bookcases and on a sideboard and a low table are two more cages. I can see they're those fancy ones, with bars twirling to make patterns of trees, leaves, twisting ivy. They're empty, the little doors swung open.

"Start looking for stuff," says Marco.

For a moment I don't move. The loud ticking of the clock and the soft flow beneath my feet make it hard to fix myself in the here and now, to know what to do. Colin is squatting with his head down.

"Come on," says Marco.

I nearly slip in shit as I go over to the sideboard. I pull open the top drawer and Marco takes a few steps towards me and shines the torch beam. Little faces look up at me. I have seen something like them on TV, the faces of shrunken tribal heads. No, they're not really faces at all. It's the light, the shadow on buttons or broken crockery. Yes, that must be it.

Marco's beam has moved away. It fixes on Colin who is down against the floor with his ear pressed to the boards.

"What are you doing?" says Marco.

"I can hear the water," says Colin.

"For fuck's sake."

I close the drawer of faces. I can hear the sea, too. It's a shallow sea flowing over sand, crowding around the rocks and pebbles. The clock must have stopped because there is only silence and the sea. Then it ticks again and it has always been ticking; only the space between each tick threatens to become an endless silence filled only by the sea.

I pull out the second drawer in the dresser.

"Just get on with it, will you>" Marco says, perhaps to Colin, perhaps to me.

He flashes the torch beam around.

"Jesus," he says, "There's nothing here."

"We should go now," says Colin.

"No," says Marco, "There's the rest of the house."

I can't see what is in the second drawer, I put my hand in.

***

The next time the phone rings it's somewhere near dawn, already there is a dull, grim light seeping into the bedroom. I should turn the phone off at night. I'll never turn the phone off at night.

"Do you remember," Colin says, wheedling amusement in his voice, "what Marco was like?"

Oh yes, I remember. The way Marco had of transforming our bored hanging about into something like a life. There were other boys to terrorise, girls to tease. We'd occupy the video machine in the local chip shop and the place would become ours.

Boys, just you be nice to the customers, yes?

Later we'd demand money from smaller kids. It was as though the whole area was a stage set for our adventures.

But all the while Marco kept us in check. Sometimes I just wanted to be away, to go home and watch TV, get a glimpse of something else. Imagine not living round here. But everyone I knew lived around here.

***

I touch the substance in the drawer and a stench makes me almost gag. It's like oil, blood and fur. My fingers wade through soft jelly and I quickly pull my hand out, wipe it frantically on my jeans.

"The sea is beneath the floor," Colin is saying. "Just below these boards."

I can hear it again, the tingle as it flows. I taste the tang of salt and the clear air you get as you approach the coast.

"Don't be a moron," says Marco. "Moron. Moron."

As I turn I can see Marco hit the torch against Colin's head, the light flickering around the room.

"Moron. Moron."

Sometimes he would do things like that. Slap us. Hit us. Kick us.

As I watch, the heavy ticking of the clock becomes louder as though it has just resumed.

Marco hoists Colin up.

"Look," he says, "there's nothing in this room. Let's check out the rest of the downstairs."

As we leave I glance down at the drawer, I can't see much without the torch. Somehow I resist the urge to plunge my fingers back in.

We spread out through the ground floor, each taking one of the three remaining doors. I go towards the back of the house. When I open the door the animal smell threatens to overwhelm me. At the same time the ticking rhythm of the clock rattles through my head, it speeds up, the ticks colliding with one another, becoming a broken pattern like scampering paws.

I can't bear the dark anymore so I switch on the light. It's a kitchen, old fashioned, with a blackened oven and wooden worktops. It is perfectly clean, almost normal. Not even any washing-up piled in the sink. At first it's as though the animal smell has gone but no, it lingers beneath a reek of disinfectant.

I focus on the marble of the sink and the smooth surfaces of the worktops. On one of these there is something it is better not to look at. So I forget it is there.

I notice the back door out to the garden is ajar. I walk over, open it wider and look out.

The silhouettes of tall ragged-edged plants beckon. I imagine running beneath their boughs as they become mighty trees. I imagine myself a tiny figure running free beneath their canopy.

"Hey." It's Colin at the door, slanted, clinging to the jamb. "I want to go home."

I think he might start crying and I almost laugh at how stupid this all is.

Then Marco is beside him, thumping him on the upper arm.

"Come on," he says.

I stay at the garden door. There is movement in the forest. Soon the moon will rise and in the play of light and shadow I can run and hunt with the others.

"Look," says Marco, "let's just get this over with, shall we?"

And this new tone, this need to cajole us, is more disturbing than any threat he could make.

We are all in the room but none of us look at the worktop. The knives there. The gory mess.

Marco shuts the garden door.

"What did you see in the other rooms?" I ask, bought back to the moment.

"Nothing. Just crap. Cages. Look I get it. House gives me the creeps too. But we can't leave with nothing can we? We'll check out the upstairs. And don't turn on any more lights."

***

"You remember the times before we met Marco?" Colin says, in another late night phone call.

"Sure."

I go along with his reminiscences.

"I suppose," he says, "all the trouble he got us into was leading up to the night in the house. He got what was coming."

"No," I say, "he didn't deserve what happened."

***

We go up the stairs with Marco leading us into the warm glow of the light up there. The smell from downstairs is here but now it is sweet, intoxicating. The ticking of the clock fades. There is another sound now. The steady rise and fall of her voice. None of us stop, run away. It is already too late. We continue our progress, timid yet inevitable, step by step we creep towards her voice.

When we reach the landing we see her through the open door at the end of the corridor and she is reading from a book.

For years afterwards I will think I hear again fragments of what she is saying. I catch glimpses when someone reads from *Great Expectations* on the radio and when the vicar intones at my mother's funeral. I recognise it when a newsreader relates in hushed words the effects of a grisly epidemic in a distant country.

She is far away but we reach her in a few steps. She turns and bestows her smile. She is not old at all. Or she is old in the way starlight is old.

***

"Perhaps you're right," says Colin, "Marco didn't deserve what happened."

"No."

"But I did. I'm getting my just deserts."

When he starts giggling I know it is time to bring the call to a close.

***

For long moments the woman is all I can see. She has turned to face me, large glistening eyes ranging over me. Something aches inside. There is a longing for her, an urge to bury myself, to be encompassed by her abundant dark hair, yielding flesh. As she holds me in her gaze I want to fall at her feet and worship, to run beneath her light. To hunt for her, to be hers only.

Then her eyes move on and I regain some sense of who I am.

The room opens out. It is much bigger than it should be. Somewhere in the shadows of its far side there might be a distant landscape. Everywhere are the fancy cages. They're huge now, as the perspective of the room alters. From behind the bars faces peer out. Animals that are not quite animals.

The woman still sits at the table with the book. On the other side of the table a toddler is seated. He is small enough so only his head above the mouth is showing. He is bald or has hair so thin he might as well be.

"You see, my pets," the woman announces to the room, "we have guests. Three boys. And one is not a very nice boy at all, is he?"

She is looking at Marco. He is on his knees.

She snaps her fingers and the toddler starts to stand in his seat. As he crawls onto the table I see attached to the child's head a body like a sodden, splintering log. There is movement all around the room, the cages are rattling.

With dizzying speed something pins Marco to the floor. It looks like the oar of a boat but it's sharpened at the tip, it arches over and then the thing it's connected to comes into view. What's sticking into Marco is one of the thing's many limbs, other limbs come out of a bloated lump of flesh.

My knees sag so I might collapse. I can't move as the thing puts more and more of its legs onto Marco. He's screaming. He's been screaming all the while. The thing is piercing him over and over. Now it taps one of its long claws at his head and then scrapes across so his hair and skin begin to peel away.

"Shall we let him keep his eyes?" the woman says, "or put them in the drawer downstairs with the spares?"

The toddler inches over the table towards me, dragging its ragged body, slime in its wake. Other things come out of shadows, out of cages. Amalgams of body parts, which should never have been put together. I can't take in the mess of human eyes, noses and snarled smiling lips. The fur sprouting from a human forehead. A cramped torso something like a gnarled hand wiggling its fingers.

I don't know how I break away but I run along the upstairs corridor that stretches out forever. Colin is shouting. He must be just behind me. He's telling me to run.

***

"I told you to run, didn't I?" says Colin on the telephone.

He's said this many times. But that's fine. I want him to have the consolation he's responsible for my escape.

"Yes," I say, "You told me to run. I'm grateful for that."

"Are you?" he says, "Are you grateful?"

"Look," I say, "I have to go now. I have to get up in the morning. Don't you?"

"Time doesn't work like that here," he says.

***

She calls to me in the corridor. The stairs should be just ahead but the confines of the house have buckled and ruptured. It is light, as though I am outside beneath a smouldering moon. I try to understand what she's saying but I only feel the pattern of her words, a throbbing through the world.

Somehow I keep running even though I want to turn back to her.

There is the heavy tick of the clock. The stairs down are just before me but I can hardly bear to move away from her now. Desire overcomes me and I know I must go to her.

I turn back and my foot skids in some filth on the floor. Colin collides with me. All along the corridor the creatures are coming, scuttling along the floor, the walls and the ceiling. I see the large bulbous head of the toddler. I should be terrified but want only to go to her. Want only to be pulled into her light.

Something pushes at me, making me stagger a few steps. Colin has his hands on me, scowling, desperate.

"Just run!" Colin says. He is more angry than scared.

There is a moment when I can hardly make sense of anything but then I'm going down the stairs, stumbling two at a time.

When I get out of the house I keep running. It's morning. Hours must have passed. I never see Marco, or Colin, again.

***

"When they came for you..." Colin begins.

"I know, you told me to run."

"No," he says, "you have to listen to me."

There's an odd tone of triumph in his voice.

"When they came for you, when I pushed you towards the stairs, it wasn't because I cared about saving you. It was because it was me who deserved to be with her."

I say nothing for a moment. Perhaps part of me has always known this.

"Was it worth it?" I say.

He laughs.

"This is a place someone like you could hardly imagine," he says. "A vast palace built on platforms over an unknown sea. You only glimpsed the tiniest fraction of it but it extends for miles, full of galleries and great halls with balconies, spiral stairs, room upon room. From the windows you can see across the waters to the forest where we hunt. We are her creatures and she is everywhere here, she is this place, this place is her."

"And what about you, Colin?"

"Oh, she is very kind to me. Kind to all of us. When I want to telephone you she allows me a mouth. Most days I have eyes. Sometimes I have Marco's eyes. She kept all his organs for us. Then we feasted on his discarded flesh."

"Where are you, Colin? How can I find you?"

But he will never answer this.

***

After a few days when Colin and Marco don't come home, the police question me. I don't hold out for long. I tell them about the house and they drive me in a squad car. We can't find it. Eventually it's decided the boys have run away. Boys like them do. I'm told not to play silly buggers. They say they might charge me with wasting their time.

I live. Drift but not enough to move away from the area. I have a job. A place to live. I have the routine of flipping burgers, grilling chicken.

In the small hours I dream of the house, its smell and the contents of its drawers, the cages and the creatures. I dream of the kitchen worktop with its knives and dissected flesh. To be cut and remade, reshaped. To be her creature. To be cramped in one of those cages, a foul little thing. This would be enough for me.

I don't understand why I can't find the house. I go back to the street or perhaps just a similar street, many times. I'll keep going back, keep searching. What I fear most is I've missed my chance.

Meet the Authors

Dan Allen is Canadian and enjoys spending time in Northern Ontario. You can find his short stories in numerous magazines, anthologies and podcasts. Visit www.danallenhorror.com to see a presentation of his published work.

His terrifying look at Alzheimer's, "Above the Ceiling," is featured in Bards and Sages collection of the Best Indie Speculative Fiction Vol. 2.

A personal favourite, "Sympathy for the Zingara," can be found in the March 2019 edition of ParAbnormal Magazine.

His terrifying story, "The Basement" (edited by Horror Zine's Jeani Rector), was published by Hellbound Books in July 2020.

You can visit Dan at www.danallenhorror.com and follow him on Facebook and Twitter at @danallenhorror. You can write to Dan at contact@danallenhorror.com

Olivia Arieti lives in Torre del Lago Puccini, Italy, with her family. She writes drama, poetry and fiction. Her stories have appeared in several magazines and anthologies including, *Enchanted Conversations, Enchanted Tales Literary Magazine, Fantasia Divinity Magazine, Forgotten Tomb Press, Horrified Press, Infective Ink, Pandemonium Press, Sirens Call Publications, Blood Song Books, Black Hare Press, Pussy Magic Magazine, Stormy Island*

Publishing, Breaking Rules Publishing, Scarlet Leaf Review, Iron Faerie Publishing, Dark Dossier Magazine, Paramour Ink Press, Raven and Drake Publishing.

Diane Arrelle has more than 350 short stories published and two short story collections: Just A Drop In The Cup and Seasons On The Dark Side. She, her sane husband and insane cat live on the edge of the New Jersey (USA) Pine Barrens (home of the Jersey Devil).

www.arrellewrites.com   FaceBook: Diane Arrelle

Justin Boote is an Englishman living in Barcelona and has been writing for five years. In this time, he has published around forty short stories in diverse magazines and anthologies, including ten for Scare Street's Night Terror series, a novelette called Badass with Terror Tract Publishing, two short story collections on Amazon called Love Wanes, Fear is Forever, Volumes 1 and 2, and numerous short stories.

He has also written a trilogy to be published in the summer and is currently finishing a five-book series, while also outlining another.

He can be found at his Facebook author page https://www.facebook.com/BooteJustin

Gary Budgen lives and works in London. His previous work has appeared in various magazines including Interzone, BFS Horizons, Morpheus Tales, Sein und Werden and the BFS Award shortlisted anthology Humanagerie from Eibonvale. His work has been in many other anthologies from publishers including Thirteen O'Clock Press, Boo Books and Horrified Press. A collection of stories, Chrysalis, is published by Horrified Press and the chapbook Fragments of Onyx by Salo Press. A full publishing history can be found at garybudgen.wordpress.com.

Dorothy Davies is an editor, writer, photographer and medium. Somehow all these things come together in her seemingly crowded leisure and work life. She is an avid kindle user and delights in writing reviews for Amazon, especially when a novel is deleted a mere 2-3 chapters in and is too badly written to be read… she retired from editing for a while to run a second hand shop, the best one on the Isle of Wight, but the thrill of finding and publishing outstanding stories became too much so she started again with the Gravestone Press imprint. She still runs the shop…

Sandra Davies eased herself from printmaking to writing when the wardrobe got full, by way of the illustrated 'Edge: curve, arc, circle', a coming-of-age tale set in Neolithic Orkney. Her current passion is directed towards exploring the relationship between DI Luke Darbyshere and his crime reporter friend and rival, Baz Rose, in a series of novels best described as love triangles with murder; the fourth of which – 'Drink With A Dead Man' – was published March 2021. Sandra was born in Essex, but has lived in Teesside for more than forty years.

Jim Dyar grew up in the deeper part of Maine and says he has always been a bit disturbed. He has been a professional ghost hunter, a comic book artist and is the author of the From the Minds of Humanity books, an Action / Humor series that caused several people to encourage him to write Horror. Most days he can be found researching the Paranormal, chatting with the voices in his head, or simply enjoying rowing on the swelling tide of human misery.

Michael B Fletcher is an Australian writer of adult and YA speculative fiction including fantasy, science fiction and horror. His first book *Kings of Under-Castle*, a series of humorous adventures featuring two rogues who live in the drains under a castle, was published by *IFWG Publishing Australia* in 2013.

Fletcher has over eighty short stories in magazines and anthologies in Australia, USA and the UK.

The first book of his fantasy trilogy, *Masters of Scent* is to be released by *IFWG Publishing Australia* in late 2022.

Fletcher has co-authored *Kat,* a YA Science Fiction currently being assessed for potential publication while *Mont of Siroc,* a YA Fantasy book is yet to be submitted.

Dona Fox writes short stories and poetry - horror and dark fantasy, infused with bits of science fiction. Coming from the Pacific Northwest, specters from the damp evergreen forests, Portland's bridges and Seattle's streets, often creep into her dark tales. Her stories are generally told by slightly mad narrators, full of sadness, who find themselves in dangerous situations where the edge of reality is always in question.

Dona's story *Walking on Water* appears in the Bram Stoker nominated anthology, The Beauty of Death vol. 2: Death by Water, published by Independent Legions, edited by Alessandro Manzetti.

She has two collections of short stories, Dark Tales from the Den and Darker Tales from the Den, both published by James Ward Kirk Publishing. Also, she has appeared in various anthologies published by James Ward Kirk and J Ellington Ashton Press publications in the United States and Horrified Press publications in the United Kingdom–and she appears in the original issue of *Cemetery Dance Magazine*.

Find out what Dona's reading and sign up for her newsletter online at www.donafox.com

Audible: https://www.audible.com/author/Dona-Fox

Amazon Author Page: https://www.amazon.com/author/donafox

Goodreads: https://www.goodreads.com/author/show/7352292.Dona_Fox

Michael H. Hanson created the ongoing SHA'DAA shared-world anthology series currently consisting of "SHA'DAA: TALES OF THE APOCALYPSE", "SHA'DAA: LAST CALL", "SHA'DAA: PAWNS," "SHA'DAA: FACETS", "SHA'DAA: INKED", "SHA'DAA: TOYS," and "SHA'DAA: ZOMBIE PARK", all published by Moondream Press (an imprint of Copper Dog Publishing). Michael's short story "C.H.A.D." appears in the Crystal Lake Publishing anthology "C.H.U.D. LIVES!", his short story "Rock and Road" appears in the Roger Zelazny tribute anthology "SHADOWS AND REFLECTIONS," and his short story "Born Of Dark Waters" appears in the Independent Legions Publishing anthology "THE BEAUTY OF DEATH 2: DEATH BY WATER." Michael also has stories in Janet Morris's Heroes in Hell (HIH) anthology volumes, "LAWYERS IN HELL," "ROGUES IN HELL," "DREAMERS IN HELL," "POETS IN HELL," "DOCTORS IN HELL," "PIRATES IN HELL," "LOVERS IN HELL," and "MYSTICS IN HELL." He has had over 100 short stories published in the fields of science fiction, fantasy, and horror, and he has written and published six collections of poetry: "AUTUMN BLUSH" and "JUBILANT WHISPERS" (Racket River Publishing), "DARK PARCHMENTS" and "WHEN THE NIGHT OWL SCREAMS" (MoonDream Press), and "ANDROID GIRL And Other Sentient Publications" and "QUARANTINE WORLD: Trapped in The Coronaverse" (Three Ravens Publishing).

Stuart Holland is the owner of Fiction4All, a golf enthusiast (especially the 19th hole) and has written in the genres of crime/mystery, thrillers and suspense, and has now turned his hand to horror. His books are available from fiction4all.com in both digital and print editions. His other interests include conspiracy theories, the Knights Templars and has a fascination for the paranormal and supernatural. Which may explain why he wrote 2020-Wipeout a couple of years before Covid-19 had ever been heard about!

Wendy Lynn Newton is an Australian fiction and non-fiction writer. She is the author of two non-fiction books, and her short stories and feature articles have appeared in many key international and Australian literary and media publications. Wendy is a Full Member of the Australian Society of Authors and spent several years as a member of Write Response, a team of independent Tasmanian arts reviewers, after being selected by Arts Tasmania for an arts@work mentorship. She is currently working on a young adult science fiction trilogy and lives in northern Tasmania with two out-of-control Chihuahuas and two indifferent cats.
wendy.newton.launceston@gmail.com
Instagram: @wendynewtonlaunceston

Rie Sheridan Rose multitasks. A lot. Her short stories appear in numerous anthologies, including Killing It Softly Vol. 1 & 2, Hides the Dark Tower, Dark Divinations, and On Fire. She has authored twelve novels, six poetry chapbooks, and lyrics for dozens of songs. She is also editor-in-chief for Mocha Memoirs Press and editor for the Thirteen O' Clock imprint of Horrified Press. She tweets as @RieSheridanRose.

Chris Rodriguez has retired from the horrors of conventional life. She now lives on the brink of inspiration in a 100-year-old cottage in Pocatello, Idaho. Her works have appeared in various themed anthologies including Rhetoric Askew, several by Horrified Press/Thirteen O'Clock, Left Hand Publisher's, *Mindscapes Unimagined*, ParABnormal Magazine, DL Russell's *Nobody Goes Out Anymore* and Blunder Woman Productions, *Wrong Turn,* which has recently won Best Audiobook Anthology at the SOVAS Awards. You can find her latest athttps://www.chrisrodriguez-onthebrink.com
or
https://www.amazon.com/author/chrisrodriguez-onthebrink.

Mark Towse is an Englishman living in Australia. He would sell his soul to the devil or anyone buying if it meant he could write full-time. Alas, he left it very late to begin this journey, penning his first story since primary school at the ripe old age of forty-five. Since then, he's been published in the likes of Flash Fiction Magazine, The Dread Machine, Cosmic Horror, Midnight in the Pentagram, Suspense Magazine, ParABnormal, and Raconteur. His work has also appeared on many exceptional podcasts such as The Grey Rooms, No

Sleep, Creepy, Tales to Terrify, etc. His first collection, 'Face the Music,' was released by All Things That Matter Press in 2020. 'Nana,' his debut novella, was published by D&T Publishing in March 2021, available via the usual outlets.

Wondra Vanian is an American living in the United Kingdom with her Welsh husband and their army of fur babies. A writer first, Wondra is also an avid gamer, photographer, cinephile and blogger. She has music in her blood, sleeps with the lights on and has been known to dance naked in the moonlight.

Wondra was a Top-Ten finisher in the 2017, 2018, 2019 and 2020 Preditors and Editors Reader's Poll, including the Best Author category. Her story, "Halloween Night," was named a Notable Contender for the Bristol Short Story Prize in 2015. She can be contacted through her website: https://www.wondravanian.com/.

Lightning Source UK Ltd.
Milton Keynes UK
UKHW042201010822
406697UK00001B/273